MW00467213

Praise for

"*The Unseen Battle* is a literary masterpiece that skillfully explores the age-old conflict between good and evil in a fresh and captivating way. In a world saturated with stories of love and struggle, this novel stands out as a beacon of originality and depth.

"Author Micah Leydorf has ingeniously woven together three distinct voices: the cunning lies of Twisttale, the celestial guidance of Ariam, and the poignant journal entries of Abby, an ordinary woman navigating the treacherous waters of a crumbling marriage. This unique narrative structure offers readers a multifaceted view of the unseen battle unfolding in the shadows of our daily lives.

"As an editor, novelist, and avid reader, I am continually searching for stories that not only entertain but also provoke thought and introspection. "The Unseen Battle" delivers on all fronts. It's a gripping page-turner that explores profound truths about faith, love, and the issues facing American believers.

"Through the lens of Abby's personal struggles, readers are invited to contemplate the spiritual warfare that surrounds us all. With every turn of the page, you'll find yourself drawn deeper into the intricate web of angelic intervention and demonic machinations, leaving you in awe of the author's ability to bring this hidden world to life.

"In *The Unseen Battle,* Leydorf masterfully reveals the evil powers seeking to destroy lives—and God's even more powerful forces to save them. Whether you're a believer seeking spiritual insight or simply a lover of well-crafted fiction, this novel is a must-read. Prepare to be captivated, enlightened, and deeply moved by this extraordinary tale of love, redemption, and the battle that rages on beyond our sight."

--Robin Patchen, *USA Today* bestselling author

"Micah's insights into the schemes of the enemy are brilliantly displayed in *The Unseen Battle*. Her captivating narrative between the voices of good and evil shatters deception and will help you discover once and for all that the enemy's only influence is between your own ears."

-- Christy Johnson, award-winning Christian writer and speaker

"This author had me at 'You imbelice!' I discovered that Micah Leydorf's take on C.S. Lewis's classic *Screwtape Letters*, is fun, engaging, and comfortably instructive. I recommend this fine new read by an author I expect to hear good things about over the next few years."

-- Carolyn Curtis, co-author of *Women and C.S. Lewis: What his life and literature reveal for today's culture*

"Riveting! *The Unseen Battle* is a flawless execution of the historical, social, political, and spiritual framework of the current state of the American church wrapped in a totally relatable story about a woman on the edge of self-implosion. It's a social analysis that is contemplative, witty, honest in a way that hurts yet so full of grace that the reader is left examining the state of their own souls in the mirror. This kind of seamless storytelling is exactly the type of novel that can steadily change the heart of a nation. What a gem this is for modern audiences!"

--Kat Lewis, speaker and culture creator

THE UNSEEN BATTLE

An Unexpected Love Story

A NOVEL BY

MICAH LEYDORF

Published by **Highlands Publishing, LLC** in Oklahoma City, OK

First printing 2023

ISBN-10:0989469271

ISBN-13: 978-0-9894692-7-2

Cover Design: Kristina Phillips

Prologue

This is a love story—with angels and demons.

Its pages make visible the unseen battle

waging all around us

for the fate of human souls.

Table of Contents

Prologue

Introduction

[Note: Some find it helpful to read the Study Questions in the back of the book before reading each chapter.]

Epilogue

Postscript

Group Study Questions

MICAH LEYDORF

"Be alert and of sober mind.
Your enemy the devil prowls around
like a roaring lion looking for someone to devour."

I Peter 5:8, NIV

MICAH LEYDORF

Introduction

For centuries humans have been fascinated by the supernatural. From Dante in the fourteenth century to Lewis and Peretti in the twentieth, authors have attempted to pull back the curtain, giving readers a glimpse of the spiritual battle waging beneath the surface of human interaction.

The Unseen Battle: An Unexpected Love Story continues that literary tradition, using a fictional story to expose the truth of Christ's upside-down kingdom. The story has three voices:

—Twisttale, a senior demon on the North American continent, corresponding with Stumbletrick, a fellow demon and recent transfer from the other side of the globe.

—Ariam, a heavenly voice instructing and encouraging Corel, a warrior angel pulled from the celestial realm for his first assignment on earth as a Guardian.

—And finally, Abby, an average 21st-century American woman whose journal entries chronicle the effects of the demons' efforts to destroy her marriage and the angels' attempts to save it.

For those who have eyes to see, beneath these voices and the story of a marriage hanging in the balance lies a deeper story with profound truths about the American church today.

MICAH LEYDORF

CHAPTER ONE

The Surprise Party

Stumbletrick,

Before you set one filthy gnarled claw on this continent, let me make one thing clear: America is mine.

While you and the other demons in the East enjoy your jihads and genocide, I and those under my tutelage have been slaving away, breaking our spiny backs in America for centuries. We have been working our talons down to the nub laying a groundwork of such nuance and sophistication that I doubt you can understand it, let alone replicate it.

Follow my instructions, but don't even think about doing anything more. I don't want morons like you interfering with the elaborate seductions in America that have taken generations to establish.

Now for your assignment. It's not difficult, but I fear your years of service in the easy evil of the East have softened your brain, if not your scales, since our time together at the academy. You weren't all that impressive then either. Still, only an idiot could fail at this point, which I suppose is why the powers below chose you. If they gave *me* carte blanche, this would be done already.

Regardless, your victim stands at the edge of a precipice. It's all cued up. It only remains for you to push her over. We have done all the heavy lifting. I would go into more detail, but you know what they say about throwing pearls before swine. I'll leave some of the work for you to do yourself.

Whatever you do, don't screw up —

Twisttale

ABBY'S JOURNAL

Friday, December 25th —

After all the weeks of planning and hard work, today's the big day—Josh's surprise birthday party. I can't wait. I've spent six months agonizing over menus, invitations, guest lists, and decorations. He's going to love it! I lost count of how many Pinterest boards I have now. I bet hosting a surprise, sit-down dinner party for fifty people on Christmas Day involves more strategy than most Civil War battles. And that's just the planning—don't even get me started on the cooking, cleaning, and decorating. Thank goodness I have Ruthie to help with that. She sure is earning her Christmas bonus this year. I don't know what people do without help. I get tired just thinking about it, but it will all be worth it tonight! You only turn fifty once, after all.

I'm still a little nervous about not going with Eden's fancy caterers and giving the job to that new single mom who barely speaks English instead. I'm hoping that good deed goes unpunished. Regardless, time for the final push! D-day.

Saturday, December 26th —

Yay! Everyone agreed it was brilliant! The surprise came off without a hitch. They loved the made-from-scratch hors d'oeuvres (whew! I gave a big tip to the caterer and will be passing her info onto my friends). Eden and Andrew raved about the decorations. I told Ruthie there's no such thing as too many twinkle lights. Everyone kept going on and on, saying they didn't know how I managed to pull off customized party favors for so many guests. Even hard-to-please Ivy made it through the evening without a single snarky comment (or maybe just one or two slight ones). I'm calling that a coup.

Lucas said it was lovely and commented on how lucky Josh is to have such a talented wife. It was kind of nice to see him a little jealous of the one who got away. I know it's a bit weird to have an ex-boyfriend at your husband's surprise party, but my oldest friend in the world Jessica asked at the last minute if she could bring him as her plus one. I find it hard to deny her anything, and at the rate she goes through men, she's probably scraping the bottom of the barrel to find any new ones.

Of course, Josh would want family there, too. The twins were home from college for winter break, so they made an appearance. I invited Josh's parents, but our friends are not exactly their scene. It would be tedious for everyone involved to hang out together for hours. So, in a stroke of genius, I only invited them to come for cake at the end, but I also asked his dad to make the toast. His dad was honored, and no one felt uncomfortable. Win-win! My cheeks ached by the end of the night from smiling and laughing so much. It was fun, but I'm glad it's over. I wonder how many points in the good wife column this will score me.

Sunday, December 27th —

"You almost ruined my birthday, Abby."

Are you kidding me? After all I've done, all my work, all that effort—*that's* what Josh said to me. I couldn't believe my ears.

To be honest, I had to pry it out of him. I hadn't expected gushing praise, of course. He's not the type. But I thought he would say or do *something*— a quiet smile of approval, maybe a few words of acknowledgment at the party, or a sincere thank you in private afterward. I don't need much. But he hadn't said anything. Not one word. I wondered what he was thinking behind his silence and tight-lipped smile. Was he upset that Lucas had come? Was he angry that I only invited his parents for dessert? Did he think I must already know how much he appreciated my efforts without him saying so? After several heavy-handed hints throughout the next day failed to produce a response, I finally asked him when we were lying in bed last night.

"So, what did you think of the party?"

He turned toward me and tucked a stray lock of hair behind my ear. "You know I love you, Abby. But was that party really for me? You were so busy getting all the details perfect that you missed the joy of being present with our friends. Honestly, you almost ruined my birthday."

Ruined his birthday? Was he kidding? I worked so hard. Of course, I did it all for him.

"You know I would have been just as happy with a fish fry. I don't need anything fancy to enjoy being with our friends and hearing about their lives, but it seemed like you wanted everyone to be impressed with all that *you* had done. You made it more about you than my birthday, honey."

Although he delivered the words gently, I couldn't have been more shocked if he had slapped me in the face.

In all our years of marriage, Josh has never said an unkind word to me. He gets frustrated at times, but I've always loved how he manages to call me out without shaming me. I guess I should be glad he didn't say anything until I asked. He's never been malicious, and he wasn't tonight. His voice was steady, not angry, but his words still crushed me.

I didn't try to defend myself. I turned away and got up to turn out the light, letting my tears fall in the darkness instead of betraying them by reaching up to wipe them away. Before saying good night, I squeezed out a few words about how putting a lot of thought and effort into an event shows that you care about the guest of honor and the guests, hoping he didn't notice the crack in my voice . . . or the breaking of my heart.

Dear Corel,

We are so very grateful you are here with our dear girl Abby. Thank you for sending your analysis of the situation along with the vial of her precious tears. Our Most Blessed Lord personally sends you his thanks for capturing them. His love for each human soul—as deep and intimate as His creation is vast and expansive—boggles even our angelic minds.

Despite this being your first assignment on earth, you show great promise. I confess I had some reservations. I know our forces in the celestial battlefield mourn the loss of your bravery and your famed sword, but warrior angels don't always make the best Guardians. It's a different skill set, you know. I had visions of you barging in with your sword swinging, ready to seize your charge, sever her chains, throw her over your shoulder, and fly her to safety. Of course, it doesn't work like that. On earth, our enemies work in secret. Guarding humans from their attacks requires finesse, patience, and restraint.

But your report assuaged my fears, assuring me that you see Abby's beauty despite her imperfections. I loved reading your description of her with her children—running out to meet them, plying them with food, and eagerly listening to their stories. Even though her nest is almost empty as they like to say, she obviously still revels in their beauty, smiles, and laughter. My favorite part was when you said she reminded you of Our Lord and how He delights in and cares for His own children.

I feared you might minimize her pain such as it is living in comfortable suburban America. Her situation probably seems trifling compared to the horrors suffered by others around the world. Still, you seemed to grasp the weight of her emotional labor and the importance of her role as a nurturer.

Even though it might seem tame to you, this mission ranks of utmost importance in the Kingdom of God. Our struggles on earth differ from the open warfare in the heavenly realm, but the stakes are just as high, if not higher. It's why Our Lord hand-picked you for this assignment. Her soul hangs by the slimmest of threads. Our enemies even now hold her in their fearsome grip. The situation continues to deteriorate, and our intelligence informs us they are preparing to strike a fatal blow.

She passed the point of praying for herself long ago—a dire case. But prayers have been lifted on her behalf, and you are their answer.

You won't need your usual battle paraphernalia. We use weapons of a different sort in our fight against evil on earth—like truth, goodness, and beauty. Teaching you how to use these powerful weapons will be part of my job. Her tears are actually a good start. The Holy Spirit is at work.

Godspeed, Corel! Remember, all Heaven is with you.

For His Glory,

Ariam

You imbecile!

Who said anything about killing her? Since when do we care if human vermin live a few seconds longer? I would think the centuries of martyrs in the East would have taught you this. They are all destined to be worm food. We don't care about *ending* their lives. That happens with or without us. We want to *ruin* their lives and, more importantly, their eternities. It's not physical pain and discomfort that kills their souls. It's the stories they tell themselves.

Human authors know this. Any achiever feels it. Put a human on a mountain, challenge him to reach the summit, and he'll trudge voluntarily up the slope, relishing the wind and ice pelting his face all the while. But put him on a couch and merely drip some water from the ceiling, and he won't tolerate it for a moment.

The difference? The narrative.

From their side of the veil, they can't distinguish fiction from reality. They simply don't have the faculties. Like the blind, they rely on other voices to make sense of their world. Make sure she's listening to *your* voice. Tell her she's on the couch, she has too far to go, she's inconsequential, she may as well sit down and rest. The possibilities are endless. Try whispering a few of these in her ear:

- you can't do it
- it's too hard
- you're too tired
- scroll on your phone
- no one cares
- it doesn't matter
- you can't fix it
- you're too old

- you're too young
- have a drink
- eat some ice cream
- take a bath
- watch a movie
- binge a show
- read the comments
- it doesn't hurt anyone

You get the idea. The truth is, of course, the exact opposite. Oh, it will hurt all right. All those small decisions she thinks are harmless will rot her insides as surely as a nest of termites munching away at the foundation of a house.

How can you be such an idiot about this? When I said push her over the cliff, I was talking about her *marriage*, you moron! That's what we cued up for you. It's on its last legs. One good shove will send it toppling into oblivion. And before you jump to any stupid oversimplifications, destroying marriages isn't always our goal. Abusive marriages sometimes actually work in our favor, but that's another story. In this case, however, destroying *her* marriage absolutely is our goal, and when this marriage comes falling down, it will take her and many others with it. That's how these things work. They are all connected—their souls, their bodies, their marriages, and those around them.

Don't judge the importance of this assignment by its lack of difficulty though. Oh, no. This case is high priority for Our Enemy Above. He claims to love even the vilest of these human maggots. It is, therefore, a high-priority mission for us as well, which is why, of course, I expressed my opposition to you being entrusted with it.

Corruption here requires subtlety and nuance. You don't have to be a genius to take advantage of the elaborate elixir of illusion we have created here in the West, but it does take only one fly in the ointment to wreck it for everyone else.

So, a word of warning (as I know you've seen the torments that can await):

Don't let that fly be you—

TwistTale

CHAPTER TWO

The Happiness Project

ABBY'S JOURNAL

Friday, January 1st —

I can't do this anymore. I can't keep trying so hard.

I guess my whirl of activities had been keeping at bay the growing emptiness inside me, but Josh's words—*"You almost ruined my birthday"*—pierced right through that facade. I can't pretend anymore. I've suspected for a while now that no matter how much I do, it will never be enough. People will still criticize. Now when I tried my hardest, the one person who supposedly loves me unconditionally said it was garbage.

My stomach hurts when I think about it too much, when I let the tapes play in my mind. I've had anxiety before, but this is different. I'm scared to get out of bed, leave the house, or talk on the phone for fear of rejection and criticism. I'm hiding on the floor of my closet crying as I write this.

I need to talk to someone. I can't talk to Josh, not unless I want to risk being cut to the bone again. I can't take that right now. Ruthie still comes to help with the house and other projects even though Cash and Destiny aren't living at home any more, but I could never confide in her.

When did conversation become such an extravagance? Friends used to talk for hours. Now, I have to ask permission to have a conversation instead of sending a four-line text. If it takes over thirty seconds of anyone's time, apparently, it's not worth it. *I'm* not worth it.

I guess everyone's billable rate has gone up and sharing life with me isn't making the cut. Blame it on marriage, or kids, or jobs, or social media. I do blame it a lot on social media...and smartphones.

I keep seeing that stupid post going around, *My door is always open. My house is safe. Coffee could be on in minutes, and my kitchen table is a place of peace and non-judgment. Anyone who needs to chat is welcome anytime....*

What a load of crap! How can they claim their doors are open when they can't be bothered to answer their phone? They couldn't find time to have coffee if I gave them two months' notice. They claim peace and non-judgement immediately after proclaiming they hate half of the country who voted differently than they did.

But I'm not interested in blame. I don't care. I only know I can't fight this tide of isolation, shame, and hostility on my own. The world feels like a very lonely place. And I'm finding I can't handle the rejection.

It's everywhere. Friends can't make time for anything more than a half-a-second to "like" a photo. Self-righteous social justice warriors wait, eager to pounce on my every move. A sea of smiling faces at church ask how I am doing but don't really care. They would be irritated and shocked to hear anything other than a quick "Good!" or "Busy!"

If I left, no one would even notice—until they needed volunteers. "Abby should be able to do it. She doesn't work full-time. What? She quit coming a year ago? Wonder why. Well, who else can we ask?"

After a thousand shallow interactions, you can only kid yourself for so long that anyone cares. So I've stopped kidding myself.

Here's the kicker, though. You know the one person who does want to talk? Lucas. He sent me a text last week after the party. *Great to see you. Love to get coffee if you ever need to talk.* I can't believe I'm even considering it. Everyone would say it's a bad idea to see an ex-boyfriend, especially Ruthie, who never makes a secret of her opinions. That's why I'll be telling her I have a dentist appointment—if I decide to go. Sometimes you just need someone to make you feel good about yourself. How bad could one cup of coffee be?

Dear Corel,

Wow, your talent as a strategist rivals your reputation as a warrior. Thank you for your detailed analysis and battle plans. You've correctly identified some key vulnerabilities, especially her obliviousness to the danger of her isolation.

But let's hold off on calling in reinforcements just yet. I know it looks bad. Believe me, I'm not minimizing the threat. You are absolutely correct that she fails to realize the strategic importance of her relationships and makes no provision for their protection. Yes, she doesn't pray for her husband or friends, becomes irritated when they don't do just what she likes, and harbors resentment instead of extending grace for their weaknesses. I share your pain over her carelessness with her marriage. It's like watching someone practice their golf swing amid the glorious stained-glass windows of Sainte Chapelle in Paris, not realizing that one slip of the club could shatter into a million pieces something that can never be replaced.

But I wouldn't overestimate this current conflict over the party and her angst about it. Our Lord sometimes paints His most glorious pictures with dark colors. Even celestial beings like ourselves can't always see which circumstances in their lives will work for ultimate good. Only Our Lord, the master conductor, can orchestrate His intricate magnum opus. Humans jump to label certain things as blessings from God, like a new job, good health, or a windfall of cash. We know, however, that sometimes the most trying of circumstances can be the best thing for a human soul—and winning the lottery can be the worst.

What matters the most right now, even more than her actual circumstances, is the story that she tells herself. Far from inconsequential or innocuous, stories can transform the routine into the holy, the ordinary into the sacred. Humans instinctively know this. They are attracted to stories from birth. From the earliest civilizations that gathered around the glow of campfires to the silver screens of Hollywood, humans are drawn to storytellers. Our Lord knew this. Think of all the wonderful stories he told. I can't decide if my favorite is the one about the good Samaritan, the lost sheep, or the prodigal son.

He, the Master Storyteller, has authored the most magnificent of all epics. It is up to us to discover how to help Abby to understand her true place in God's beautiful story. She needs to know that she is part of a greater plan, a glorious romance in fact. She is Our Lord's beloved, His precious prodigal child, the wayward lamb that He leaves the flock to search for and find, who He rescues, binds up, and carries back in His arms.

Right now, our enemy has her trapped in self-pity, blinded by a false narrative that she is alone and unloved. Little does she realize her thoughts, decisions, and actions affect far more than just herself and her husband. How do we help her see the vital role she plays in bringing the kingdom of God to earth? It's not the sort of thing accomplished in a weekend.

In the meantime, I know you will stay by her side, even if that means allowing her to walk into some coffee shops where you don't think she should go. You can guard her from some harm, but even Our Lord had to walk through the wilderness. I'm afraid these difficulties only mark the beginning of some very dark valleys for Abby, but they might also be the best way for her to reach the glorious light on the other side.

Our unceasing prayers are with you as you help Abby walk through this darkness.

For His Glory,

Ariam

Stumbletrick,

If you say "in the East, we do such and such" one more time, I'm going to carve a W on your tongue so you'll remember where you are. I don't care how you do it over there!

Here in the West, we don't need physical jail cells, censors, or secret police to imprison and indoctrinate our prey. Those techniques are for amateurs—blunt instruments for feeble-minded tempters. We stock our arsenals with more sophisticated devices like habits, addictions, and rationalizations. She cannot escape from the prison of her own mind or the net that she, with her seemingly harmless habits, winds tighter every day. The lies that blind the most are the ones she tells herself: *I just need a glass of wine to help relax. A new dress will make me feel better. Scrolling through social media doesn't really melt my brain.*

Make yourself scarce. Or rather, make sure she doesn't recognize your presence in those little distractions, redirections, or gentle nudges down the path to her own glorious destruction. Or you'll find yourself begging for the relief of your own prison cell.

Don't tell me how to torture —

Twisttale

ABBY'S JOURNAL

Saturday, January 2nd —

Happiness, here I come!

Enough with the self-pity, already. That's not going to get me anywhere, so I broke down and hired a life coach, bought a journal from Gretchen Rubin's *Happiness Project*, and now I just need to decide what my happiness commandments will be. Gretchen did twelve commandments, one for each month of the year, but that sounds like a lot and a long time to wait to be happy. Tackling four commandments simultaneously instead until Easter seems like a better fit for me. I told my life coach, and she assures me that four months should be enough time (which is good because that's all I can afford now that I'm reduced to paying people to listen to me).

1. *Pay attention to what I pay attention to.*

I'm not sure what that even means, but my life coach told me to, so that's number one. Based on my super depressing entry yesterday, I'm not sure that one is going to work. But if I'm going to pay for advice, I figure I should take it, so I'll give it a go.

2. *Act the way I want to feel.*

I have more hope for this one.

Gretchen says we need concrete, measurable steps for each commandment, so my concrete plan for commandment #1 is to pay more attention is journaling! If too many screens, too much scrolling, and too much busyness got me here feeling alone and rejected even when I'm with people—or *especially* when I'm with people—slowing down and doing something creative instead of consuming content might be the way back.

First baby step on commandment #2: Can't wait until Easter!

Monday, January 4th —

I already missed a day of journaling. Dang it. Why can't I be better? Maybe for the same reason I couldn't even keep myself from eating that five-day-old cinnamon roll or prying some stale candy from the gingerbread house last night. And then hinting it must have been one of the twins when Ruthie asked about it. Oh well, back to making progress on my commandments. I decided on the third one.

3. *Remember things that bring me joy.*

For our session tomorrow, my life coach asked me to write about why I married Josh in the first place. I remember the first time I saw him. It was on the Tube when I was working in London during the early-morning commute. Everyone else was stony silent, absorbed in a book or on a phone, half asleep or thinking about their days, all politely ignoring one another except to move out of the way as bodies entered or exited the train. Everyone except Josh.

He chatted with a little boy who was seated across the aisle from him. The kid was probably on his way to school or daycare, riding with his parents. From the seat behind, I listened to the childish chatter and the intriguing stranger's gentle, encouraging responses. The cadence of their voices broke the monotony of the train swooshing through the tunnels. I don't remember what they were talking about. I find it hard to pay attention to what five-year-olds say, let alone remember almost twenty years later. But I remember the boy's happy chatter, his shining eyes looking up at Josh's dark ones.

I marveled at a full-grown, seemingly intelligent man oblivious to what anyone else around him might be thinking, smiling and laughing at the enthusiastic ramblings of a child as if there were nowhere else in the world he'd rather be. It melted my heart. Who does that? Who was this guy? Who sent him down to earth?

I was smitten from the moment he looked my way after the boy and his parents exited the train. I never had a chance. Strangely enough, I don't remember what he said to me either, except it wasn't some cheesy pick-up line. I remember how he moved, his easy smile, his comfortable laugh, and how I felt—like I couldn't believe this incredible guy was talking to me. He was so different from everyone else. When he invited me out, wild horses couldn't have kept me away.

That feeling only deepened as I got to know him.

But that was a long time ago. It's hard to remember now when we lie side-by-side in bed each night not touching, hardly talking, and wondering how we got here. I can't even keep the tears from falling on these pages as I think about how lonely I feel with him now compared to what I'd hoped for back then.

Yep, that's the worst.

Tuesday, January 5th —

Boy, I sure did open the flood gates in hiring that therapist..., I mean life coach. But it's definitely helping me with that first commandment about paying attention. She's got me telling her stuff I don't tell anybody (or even admit to myself)—like how desperately I needed Josh at first.

I used to brag about him all the time. When you're in love, you do stupid things like not realizing how idiotic you sound telling everyone about how your boyfriend/fiancé/husband saved you from your destructive self.

I had everything that supposedly makes life worth living—prestigious job at a publishing house, nice flat, lots of acquaintances, a few friends, even good sex. But I was miserable.

I was dying inside. Sounds dramatic and cliché, I know. But what would you call it when you're so lonely you can't help fantasizing mid-conversation about going upstairs and opening up your wrists in the bathtub? It's hard to argue that it's a good place to be.

I had the dream—everything the world around me told me I wanted—but I wasn't happy. I was only busy. I was achieving career goals. I was entertained. I was comfortable, but my soul thirsted for more. Jim Carrey once said he wished everyone could get rich and famous and have all they dreamed of so they could see it wasn't the answer. I may not have been as successful as him, but I was successful enough to realize all that stuff doesn't bring peace or joy.

I'm glad I met Josh when I did. I wouldn't have given it all up before then. The dream had the greatest stranglehold on me while I was still striving for it. Once I achieved it, it turned to sand in my hands like the mirage that it was.

And that was exactly when he appeared, when I was ready to throw my life away. On that subway car watching Josh talk to that little boy... it was like the heavens opened and dropped Josh in my lap. He wasn't like anyone else. I can admit he's not classically handsome. His skin, hair, and eyes are all dark, his nose a tad oversized. No sparkling blue eyes, no chiseled jaw, no rippling muscled shoulders. No one would ever mistake him for a movie star. And I usually don't like a guy with a beard.

But there's something incredibly attractive about the gentleness he showed that boy, the confidence he displayed in not caring what anyone else thought, and the boldness and simplicity in his eyes when he looked at me and said, "Let me buy you dinner."

I loved that. No pussyfooting around. No hedging his bets. No wishy-washy "some folks are going out for drinks" or "wanna grab a bite?" I didn't have to wonder if he was asking me out on a date or if I was hungry. His words were a simple invitation I couldn't resist.

So, we went to dinner. The other guys I'd been casually dating never entered my mind. It didn't feel like cheating. It felt like melting. I'd been so resistant to commit when they pressured me, but after Josh kissed me on our very first date and said, "You can tell them you're only dating me now," I happily assented, "Okay."

The years of striving—dating and strategizing and playing little games of one-upmanship—all disappeared as I leaned into this man who eschewed it all. He's not smooth. He's been known to ask awkward questions. He is honest and direct. And different. He exudes peace and quiet strength, and the man doesn't have a frantic bone in his body. But the most appealing of all—what was so different from anyone else I'd ever met—is the deep joy he carries through life, as if he already has what everyone else is trying so hard to get. Back then, when I was with him, when I sat close against him in the booth at dinner, or held his hand in the park, or stood by his side at a party, that same peace and joy rubbed off on me.

It didn't feel like I decided to marry Josh. It felt more like he swooped in and rescued me. I had reached the end of my old life and was more than happy to trade it all in for this most extraordinary person—who amazingly chose to love me and invited me into his world.

Dear Corel,

Well done, soldier! Excellent job adjusting your battle plans to meet Abby's real need—someone who will listen and point her toward the true, good, and beautiful. Your work with the counselor will help her more than your flaming sword right now.

On this side of the veil, their fragile bodies and minds can't process Our Lord's full glory, or even ours, any more than they can stare directly into the sun. Instead, Our Lord teaches humans about His love and infinite grace by developing their faith in the unseen.

Though we rarely appear or intervene physically on earth, we do provide aid constantly. We listen to their prayers, even the unspoken ones. We observe and bear witness to their stories—their sufferings, pain, joy, and gratitude. In doing so, we acknowledge their worth. We form part of that great cloud of witnesses cheering them on in their race to the finish. This is no small contribution.

Here's a little secret: the human soul longs to be seen and known (and soothed once she will let us), as much, if not more than being advised or rescued.

You're doing great.

For the Glory of Our Lord,

Ariam

Stumbletrick,

What is your strategy here? Does letting her stroll down memory lane until she remembers all the reasons she first fell in love with her husband sound like a good way to drive a wedge between them to you? I wish I could send you to the torturers right now, you fool.

I know you can't commandeer her thoughts. I'm not asking you to possess her therapist exorcist-style and dictate commands, but I assumed you had a scrap of creativity in that wart-covered head. My mistake was to expect rudimentary competence from you.

You have a tool at your disposal, one that's so obvious it's almost a trope. Instead of sitting alone with her journal, how about getting her out and about. Specifically, how about an "innocent" coffee with that "old friend" who has been texting her?

Your stupidity astounds me —

Twisttale

CHAPTER THREE

Lucas

ABBY'S JOURNAL

Saturday, January 9th —

I made progress on my happiness project. I decided on my last commandment: *Connect meaningfully with others.*

So I saw Lucas yesterday. We met in one of those hipster coffee shops with the exposed brick walls and comfy couches that are so easy to sink into, but I wonder how often they have been cleaned. I allowed myself to indulge in a steaming chai tea latte but held off on the salted caramel cake pop. One has to draw the line somewhere.

I had been ignoring his texts, not only because he was an old boyfriend, but also because Jessica had invited him to Josh's surprise party. That girl is a force to be reckoned with. As if her chestnut mane and gorgeous curves that turn every head in the room weren't enough, she also has an over-the-top, crazy-fun personality that has kept the boys fixated since way back in junior high. I learned early it wasn't worth it to challenge her or step on her toes—better to sit back and enjoy the ride.

But last week, the thought popped into my head that maybe *because* Jessica was dating Lucas, that made it okay for us to get coffee. It's not like he's single. We're both with someone else now. Maybe I really could have a meaningful connection with an old friend.

Of course, the conversation came around to Josh. I tried to be reticent like a good wife should be, but once the dam was breached, I couldn't stop the complaints from flooding out like a river. Lucas didn't seem to mind the oversharing.

"He doesn't appreciate you," he agreed. "You are amazing! I can't believe he treats you that way. Did he really say you ruined his birthday after all your work and that spectacular party you threw for him?"

His smooth words soothed my wounded ego. I metaphorically leaned into them until I found myself *literally* leaning into him on the cozy sofa. Until one comment struck home.

"You know, Abby, it doesn't sound like Josh even *likes* you."

That knocked the wind right out of me. I felt like a child twirling on the monkey bars who suddenly lost her grip and landed flat on her back. I sat up straight, so shocked that I couldn't speak or breathe, my mouth hanging dumbly open.

Lucas jumped into the silence just as he had always done when we were dating. "I never tried to change you—not your stubbornness, not your spirit. I *like* your flaws. They make you more interesting. A strong man is not afraid of a challenge, and you know I appreciate a good fight every now and then." He grinned and looked as if he hoped I'd recall some of the good-natured tussles we'd had back in the day.

I choked on my latte and set the mug on the table. Totally misreading the room, he slid his hand up my back and let it rest on my neck.

Wow, did he overshoot that one. Until then, I'd been all cozy, telling myself there was nothing wrong with taking solace in the warmth and kindness of an old friend. So what if our thighs were touching? That's just physics when you sat on those old sofas. But the touch of his hand on my neck shot through me like lightning.

My power of speech returned enough to mumble, "I need to go." I struggled against the overstuffed feather cushions, gravity, and the too-familiar smell of his cologne. Ever suave and unembarrassed, he stood without effort, helped me to my feet, and said he'd had fun catching up.

His "hope to see you again soon" followed me as I rushed out the door.

Dearest Corel,

No.

You can't physically harm any humans, even the ones who might pose a risk to your charge. I know humans like to paint portraits of guardian angels as maternal-looking robed figures with wings hovering over children, presumably to bat away threats. They talk about how their guardian angel must be worn out from knocking their charges out of the way of reckless cars or their own stupidity, but that's not how it works.

We aren't nearly as concerned with physical danger or suffering as we are about the state of their souls. Inflicting damage to Lucas' body wouldn't protect our girl from her real danger or advance our mission, no matter how cathartic it might feel.

That doesn't mean, however, that we let him run amok.

Yes, by all means, keep her away from him. I love how a single mom once described guardian angels as big tough Secret Service agents in suits with earpieces and a hand on their charge's elbow to guide them—and maybe even carry them a little through the difficulties of each day. Even though it's not technically accurate, there is a fair bit of truth and beauty in that image.

Focus on Abby, not Lucas. Guide her where she needs to go—toward a more truth-filled narrative about her marriage. Throw out an elbow or two at Lucas if needed, but let others sort him out. If we can help open Abby's eyes to the beauty in front of her, we won't need to worry about Lucas or any other temptations that might emerge.

Human marriages are so much more than a solemn promise, convenient social agreement, or the foundation of the family unit. They are a sacrament. As one wise priest once wrote, each marriage is "a book of God written in flesh." Our diversity-loving Lord designed humans so they can grasp the depths of His grace in an infinite number of beautiful ways, but marriage is one of my (and His) favorites. Which is part of why we are fighting so hard for this one.

Remember, we are praying for you and yearning for your success.

For His Glory,

Ariam

Stumbletrick,

You are such an imbecile! You don't even know victory from defeat. If you expected her to hop into bed with her old boyfriend after one coffee date, you don't know your audience. That's not going to happen and wasn't ever the plan. She's way too goody-goody for something so obvious. She cares too much about what everyone else would think.

In fact, something like that could work to our Enemy's advantage. She might see the grass isn't greener, beg Josh's forgiveness, and experience anew the putrid love and grace we work so hard to snuff out. Stranger things have happened.

I'm trying to decide if the East softened your edge or if you have always lacked basic competence. Maybe the ease of your assignment camouflaged it all these years. Whatever the case, you need to set those beady eyes a little farther down the road than the end of your crooked nose. We're playing the long game here. We don't have to whip her around 180 degrees when nudging her two degrees off course would suffice. She'll still end up far from her desired destination over time. In fact, subtlety is superior because she doesn't realize where she's heading.

Don't over-think it and, for crying out loud, don't try to show off. A cup of tea can distract her from prayer just as well as a gin and tonic. Stay focused, you blithering fool. You don't need to make her an alcoholic (as much fun as addiction is) or in this case push her toward a one-night stand.

Remember the goal: drive a long-term wedge between her and her husband. That comment about Josh not liking her—that is the gold here. That low-life louse basically planted a field of land mines in your victim's brain waiting to be exploited, and you don't even realize it.

I better see some bloody explosions in the near future or the collateral damage is going to be you.

Do better or else —

Twisttale

CHAPTER FOUR

Ivy

ABBY'S JOURNAL

Monday, January 11th —

I'm so upset I haven't been able to concentrate on anything since my coffee with Lucas, so I plopped down at the kitchen table and called Ivy. (For the record, I'm calling that another concrete step forward on my happiness commandment #4 of connecting meaningfully with others.)

"You know I've always thought Josh was boring," Ivy intoned, never one to mince her words. I'm not sure why I called her except that I couldn't exactly call Jessica, considering she's been *seeing* the guy who just made a pass at me. "I've never understood what attracted you to him. He's completely unimpressive."

"Good grief, Ivy. Remember, you're talking about my husband."

"We don't need men at all, but if you're going to have one, at least it should be someone intellectually and physically stimulating. Josh has never struck me as either." I could picture her on the other end of the phone, her straight hair pushed behind her ear, her glasses—which I had never been convinced weren't just for show—perched on the end of her nose. We'd met in college. I'd done the normal four-year stint, and she'd never left, moving straight into her Master's degree, then her Ph.D., now a tenured professor of women's studies.

"This is not helpful," I complained, wishing that I hadn't called.

"Oh, is truth not helpful? Sorry for being the friend who calls it as I see it. I'm not going to compromise my integrity by saying less than I believe."

I laid my forehead on the table and my phone on speaker next to my ear.

"Your truths exhaust me." I sighed. "I need alcohol to absorb them, and I don't have any right now, so I'm going to let you go." I didn't wait for her response before I hung up the phone. I might need to do an exercise a la the life coach to remember why I'm friends with Ivy as well as why I fell in love with Josh.

Why did I fall in love with Josh?

It wasn't his looks, and it wasn't his money. His father is loaded, but Josh didn't have any. Coming from a super wealthy background gives a person a certain boldness and confidence that I didn't have. That was part of it, I think. But what drew me to him the most was his commitment—right from the start with no hesitation, like God gave him an inexplicable, unconditional love for me. I'm not sure *what* made him fall head over heels, but he never made it a secret that he had.

Opposites attract, I guess. My family came from nothing. I had to scrape and fight for anything and everything. No one was going to hand me my future on a silver platter, or even twenty bucks for pizza. I had to earn it. I couldn't rest on a family name or fortune. Ivy insists there's no such thing as destiny or providence, but I can't help but think there was something beyond ourselves that brought Josh and me together.

I was nervous the first time I met Josh's dad. I had envisioned an imposing silver-haired old man with a Charlton Heston voice, or maybe a slick Gordon-Gecko tycoon in an Armani suit. He was neither. I don't know why I didn't think he would resemble his son.

He was in his garden with a well-worn walking stick in his hand, his face shaded by an old broad-rimmed sun hat. When Josh and I came around the corner, his face lit up. He opened his arms wide, and he and Josh embraced like they hadn't seen each other in years instead of weeks. I'm not all that comfortable with public displays of affection, so I was a little worried about what awaited me.

Thankfully, he only gave me a warm smile and an enthusiastic, "Abby! We've been looking forward to meeting you! Come, see my roses before the sun sets." He took my hand, placed it on his arm, and guided me through the maze of plantings. I silently wondered how he got to be so wealthy without more of a cut-throat edge.

The gravel path crunched beneath our feet as he pointed out the brilliant blossoms and the tiny delicate ones that some might overlook. In no hurry at all, he insisted we sit under a vine-covered bower, breathing in the perfume of the honeysuckle and watching the changing colors of the sky until they disappeared.

Then the lights of the house and the savory aroma of a roast coming from the kitchen beckoned us through the open patio doors to a long wooden table set with decanters of red wine and half dozen different cheeses, nuts, dried fruits, and cured meats.

As the main courses were brought from the kitchen, he pulled out a chair next to his own and said, "Please sit here beside me, Abby." I worried, thinking I was in the hot seat. But I couldn't have been more wrong.

I still return to my memory of that dinner for a scrap of hope when I am downhearted. I don't remember a single solitary word exchanged across the table or what even what was served, but I remember being enveloped in laughter and conversation. For once, I forgot all about how I might be perceived and simply felt blessed to be included. And as I watched Josh's dad preside over the feast with joy and ease, I couldn't shake off a strange feeling that I'd seen him somewhere before.

As we left that evening, I hung on to Josh's hand as it draped around my shoulder. I could still hear the splash of the fountain on the patio that mixed with the now fading chatter and laughter. I said to Josh, "No wonder you're the way you are."

"How is that?"

"So confident. So peaceful. So full of joy. How could you be otherwise when you come from all of this?" I gestured at the brick arches lining the front courtyard as we walked down the long winding driveway toward his car.

"You could be all those things, too, Abby."

"Too late for me. Our brains and hearts soak up all this stuff when we're young, internalize all the messages, create or disconnect all those neural pathways that make us who we are."

"People change." He smiled down at me. "I've seen it happen."

"I'm not sure they do. Plus, I don't have to be like you, right? Can't we just appreciate our differences? That's what makes the world go round. You can be the peaceful, loving, idealistic one who tells our kids to turn the other cheek. I can be the feisty realist who takes the bullies aside and threatens to beat them within an inch of their lives if they don't leave my family alone." I laughed. "I can't be all laid back and comfortable in my own skin. You're stuck with the performing-to-prove-my-worth person that I am."

"Our kids, huh?" He raised his eyebrows.

"Our *theoretical* kids."

"I hear marriage changes people," he suggested.

"I'm sure it does."

"Maybe we should try it."

I tried to feign indifference at his mention of marriage, despite all the blood rushing to my head. I retorted cavalierly, "I wouldn't want to marry someone who would try to change me" while inwardly steeling myself against the hope rising in my chest that he would change everything.

"Really?" He let his arm drop from my shoulder and took my hand. "You wouldn't want someone who would fill your life with love, peace, and joy? Someone who wanted to help you become all that you were created to be, your best and fullest self?"

When he put it that way... "I guess a little change wouldn't hurt."

"It wouldn't be just a *little* change. It would be everything. I give you my everything, and you give me your everything. Every day. Forever."

We had stopped walking. He pulled me around facing him, his hands encircling my waist. The full moon lit his face almost as clearly as the candlelight had over the dinner table. His brown eyes no longer twinkled with mirth. They were gentle and kind, but firm and earnest.

"I love you, Abby. Will you marry me?"

Did he really just say that? I could hear my heart pounding in my ears now.

"We haven't known each other very long...." I stammered. He reached down, took my head in his hands, and kissed me, and suddenly none of my objections mattered. I didn't care that I hadn't known him very long. I didn't care what had to change.

At that moment, I wanted him, his whole beautiful world, and everything he offered. I wanted with all my heart to be part of this family, to belong at that table, to know I would always be welcomed and that there would always be a place for me. I'd happily toss away everything else if necessary.

Back then, I hadn't been logical. I didn't make a list of pros and cons on a spreadsheet. He chose me, and I chose him. I thought I'd be eternally grateful.

I would have followed him to the end of the earth. In fact, I kind of did. For heaven's sake, I gave up a chance to stay in England and moved with him to the East Coast instead. If that's not love, I don't know what is. But I never looked back, not for a second. Not even when we lived in a tiny shoebox of a house the first year. It was so drafty and cold that first winter that I thought I'd never be warm again, but we'd just snuggle closer at night on our twin mattress on the floor, and I'd thank God again this wonderful man had chosen me.

Now we live in a great big house in the middle of the country. We have raised two beautiful children and enjoy the financial resources to do most of the things we want (including hiring Ruthie to help with the twins). But I miss those days when I never doubted Josh's love. When I talk to him now, it feels like an information dump between appointments on my part while he politely counts the seconds until he can get back to whatever he was doing. We sleep on opposite sides of a giant king bed, waking and sleeping on our own schedules.

I know it's not all his fault. I'm not that doe-eyed girl who thinks he hangs the moon anymore. I don't sit at his feet and marvel at his every word. Actually, I can't believe that I ever literally did. (Ivy must never know. She'd never let me hear the end of it.) I have my interests, and he has his. And for the most part, I'm actually okay with that.

What I can't bear is the weight of his criticism. I feel it in every single comment. That's probably why I avoid too much conversation. Again, it's at least half my fault.

When he asks, "Is it make-your-own dinner night tonight?" perhaps he's not secretly judging my lack of culinary creativity.

Maybe "Why do you need ten pairs of black shoes?" is good-natured jibe or an honest fashion inquiry.

And "What did you do today?" could be an effort to connect even if it feels like an interrogation.

At least he hasn't commented on my weight.

Dear Corel,

I love how you used dear misguided-but-oh-so-passionate Ivy's extreme views to turn Abby back in the right direction—toward Josh and the beauty and goodness of their marriage. Excellent technique—worthy of your reputation as a warrior and a great sign that you are already mastering this new field of battle as well.

Of course, she would benefit most from quiet meditation, scripture reading, and prayer. In the silence, humans can better feel the presence of the eternal and sift through all the voices to find the best way forward. But she is not choosing much quiet time at the moment.

So we need to look at other options. Those only scratch the surface of our repertoire. Longing and desire are good. Beauty—it could be as simple as a sunrise—that stirs the deeper parts of her soul and makes her long for something more can help wake her from the stupor of complacency and pull her toward the divine.

Deep down, she knows the Father Above created her for more. All humans have an innate desire to connect the present of their days with the forever of Heaven. Our enemy wants her to forget her identity. Rather than tempt her into outright evil, he diverts her focus into comfort and complacency. He wants her to see her life as a problem to be solved instead of a beautiful creation being formed.

Our job is to remind her who she is and what she was made for—just like you did with those precious memories of her first meeting with Josh and his family. Excellent work! That is who she is: beloved, desired, valued, and an honored member of the family who belongs at the table. That might be the most beautiful and powerful way that humans experience God's love—through other humans.

Fortunately, we are not limited to memories alone, even beautiful ones. Our Lord's beauty shines through all of His creation, despite the efforts of our enemies to distract and confuse!

Earth is like a giant playground where we can show humans God's truth and beauty in infinite ways if they only have eyes to see and ears to hear. Take, for example, sex and marriage. Our Lord created a framework where humans could feel the joy of family, community, and sacrificial love in order to give them a glimpse on earth of the full agape love that awaits them in the Kingdom of Heaven. As one dear saint observed about the sacramental nature of human bodies, "They make the invisible visible." Well said, John Paul.

Or food. God didn't have to create beings who need to eat in order to live. He could have designed humans to soak up nutrients from nature like plants do. Instead, they have this gorgeous, rich symbol every day of their need for Him and for one another. No wonder Our Lord called himself the Bread of Life. Our enemy has twisted this amazing gift, using it to shame and shackle our dear girl, but her memory of the wonderful feast with Josh's family gives me hope we might reclaim it.

And think about children. New humans could have hatched out of pods fully formed. Instead, He gives them adorable helpless versions of themselves that they instinctively love and want to protect and nurture. In doing so, He reveals to them previously unimaginable joy while simultaneously teaching them a level of patience and self-sacrifice that seeps down into their bones. Even the most broken versions of this relationship contain such power and beauty, and always the possibility for redemption! I love that you saw that from the very beginning with Abby.

I apologize for getting a little carried away, but as you can see, truth and beauty surround her—in nature, her marriage, her body, her children— even in her pain. She no longer sees these truths, but at least she once did.

Reminding her is a great start. Let's see if we can build on that. Our Lord is a God of re-creation who can make all things beautiful. He will work all things together for good in the end.

For His Glory,

Ariam

Shut up, Stumbletrick!

Your questions and observations are so moronic, I can hardly stand it. Your generation of demons makes me question the future of evil. Buckle up, junior, because I hardly even know where to start with your re-education.

First, you asked why do we let them have so much wealth? *That's* what you're concerned about—how big her house is, or how much money she spends, or how much food they waste? Where do I even start? Can you not see the pain leaking from every pore of her being? Yet you are hung up on how many gadgets and shoes she has?

You look at this tour de force that is America today—centuries of our carefully crafted lies woven together into a seamless whole—with all the sophistication of a cave dweller. They are miserable. They are lonely. They are killing themselves. Their pursuit of wealth pushes them away from Our Divine Enemy. But all you see are modern hospitals, shiny gadgets, big houses, fast cars, and tables of plenty?

These luxuries you bemoan are the tools of their destruction. How dense can you be not to see that? Remember that whole thing about "easier for a camel to go through the eye of a needle than a rich person to enter heaven?" This weak-mindedness is why I'm opposed to the transfer of demons from the Eastern hemisphere. Maybe you should stick with what you know—child soldiers, sex slavery, forced starvation, totalitarianism—undiluted, straight-forward evil. Leave the seduction of the West to more advanced, sophisticated minds.

Second, no, I'm not concerned about her mindlessly going to church, all her do-gooder activities, or her "happiness commandments." I swear you have the depth of a fruit fly. Those are all counterfeits—convincing substitutes for the real deal. Frankly, it's embarrassing that you don't know that without me telling you.

Your ridiculous letter has me convinced you're not contributing to her descent at all. She's simply coasting down the path your predecessors, including myself, prepared long ago for humans all across America, aided by the occasional push from her oh-so-helpful friends.

So, about her friends. I know you think you planted those seeds of resentment toward her husband, but I think it's more likely they sprang from years of conversations with friends like Ivy. Do all you can to encourage interaction with that girl and fan the flames of Abby's love-hate relationship with her. She is a fine product of a system I have worked long to perfect—American academia.

Academia, of course, isn't unique to this continent, but I have done impressive work with it here. You see, it's dangerous when the humans are smart—well, at least more intelligent than their fellow lowly bipeds. But just as with the wealth you object to, there are both pros and cons to dealing with humans with higher cognitive function.

The cons can be disastrous. Inestimable damage has been done over the centuries by some of our well-known enemies like the Apostle Paul, Saint Augustine, and even that irritating Oxford professor Lewis. But despite these exceptions, academics can be brought down quite easily and are often very useful to us. A few still resist and try to use logic to push back darkness, but I feel even they must succumb soon against the tidal wave we have set into motion.

Most intellectuals, for all their strengths, have a glaring vulnerability— pride. It is their kryptonite, to use the human vernacular. This simple but powerful weapon can bring down almost any single individual, but why leave it there? It's so much more fun to use the inflated egos, confusing doublespeak, and condescending jibes of these privileged few to inflict pain and deepen alienation from our Divine Enemy.

My decades of work in the university system are paying off handsomely. No longer content with dry journal articles, the warmth of their own mutual admiration societies, and their sense of superiority over the masses, many professors and even some students now have their own personal megaphones through social media and technology. I've made sure they measure their worth and overcompensate for their insecurities by using those channels to incite outrage in others while broadcasting their own misunderstanding of the spiritual realm. How hilarious and ironic that opponents call it virtue signaling.

I'm probably wasting my breath explaining all this to you, though. It's a couple of levels above your pay grade and your comprehension. Don't worry your ugly little head with understanding it all.

Instead, let's review your primary objective, as you seem to keep losing sight of it. Destroy her marriage! Its destruction has infinitely more strategic significance than a momentary lapse of fidelity or any other boilerplate capitulation that you might be planning. Surely your training included warnings about this dangerous institution?

Yes, relationships between the sexes can create all sorts of hurt, suffering, and abuse whether they are married or not. I didn't need you to point that out in your last letter. I am well aware that married couples can be counted among the most lonely, isolated, and miserable of humans. But you don't realize what a risky bet we would be waging by ignoring the dangers of this strategic bond.

Our Divine Adversary created marriage. It was his ultimate design even before the fall. All that rubbish about "It's not good for man to be alone" and "Woe to him who is alone when he falls." Even a neophyte like you can recognize the power of the Enemy as three and one together.

Regardless of the pain some of these unions cause, the joining of two souls together in marriage makes them exponentially more dangerous in a similar way. When used properly, marriage is almost impenetrable to us. "A threefold cord is not quickly broken," as that despicable prophet said. We need to do everything we can to prevent that. We want to attack the marriage bond in as many ways as possible—physically, emotionally, mentally, sexually—but especially spiritually.

Two equally-yoked believers pulling together focused on advancing the kingdom of Heaven while encouraging and supporting one another can accomplish exponentially more than they could accomplish alone. Not only that, they can raise up the next generation. Like the Spartan phalanx at Thermopylae—three hundred warriors repelling wave after wave of thousands of Persians, each soldier shielding the man to his left. In the same way, a united family can be virtually untouchable. And a strong family rests on the bedrock of a strong marriage. Never underestimate its power.

Together they are strong. That's why we divide them (inside or outside of marriage). Get our victims alone, and they are no match for us. Attacking them when they're inside that fortress of koinonia or true community only makes them more unified and tightens their bonds with one another. We made that mistake in the first few centuries of the church. Look what happened—it expanded around the globe. We fed them to lions for entertainment. We burned them like torches at Roman parties. But Our Divine Adversary is cunning. While we celebrated, He knew. He knew how He was establishing the foundations of His eternal army, and we were unwittingly helping Him. He knew that our attacks would unify them, that the martyrs would receive glory in Heaven.

I still wonder what would have happened if we had sown division instead. Let their ministries flourish—no beatings by the Sanhedrin, no imprisonment, no stonings. Then used our more subtle weapons like jealousy, comparison, pride, and judgment to separate them and pick them off one by one. Perhaps we could have neutralized them two millennia ago. It makes me sick to think about it.

So no more stupid questions. Just follow orders. Snap those bonds. Lure her out. Separate her from those who would protect and support her. Amplify the voices that create division. Convince her there is no danger, no threat. Trust me. Isolation is your best bet—in marriage, families, churches, and friendships. Divide then conquer. And in case you don't know how to do that, let me spell it out for you slowly: erode her trust, question his love, convince her she knows better.

Is any of this ringing a bell? If not, I really need to send a letter and have the devil in charge of training hung by his toenails and Genesis 3 reintroduced into the curriculum.

Dumbing it down as much as possible—

TwistTale

P.S. As Ivy seems to be too much for you to handle, try Eden next time. Hint: Isn't that television show, *The Bachelor*, on tonight?

CHAPTER FIVE

Eden

ABBY'S JOURNAL

Tuesday, January 12th —

Finally getting a little momentum on my happiness project! Lots to report back to my life coach in our meeting tomorrow.

Now that I'm paying attention, I'm thinking that maybe Lucas is right. Maybe Josh doesn't like me. He certainly doesn't enjoy doing the same things that I do.

Sometimes I wish Josh were more like Andrew. Not only does he not give Eden grief about her amazing shoe collection, but when they watch *Real Housewives* together, he comes up with even snarkier quips than she does. I can't imagine Josh ever doing that, let alone sending me hilarious memes, making *Bachelor* predictions, or any of the other fun things Andrew does. I know Josh has absolutely no interest, but it would be nice if he at least *pretended* he did.

Half the time, he's not even home. He's out talking to the neighbors, or with his buddies, with his family, or any variety of other places I have no desire to go (like taking the kids to all their activities when they were younger). Like I say, he has his interests, and I have mine. Is it possible to admire a quality and also find it irritating? Because Josh has a lot of those. For instance, he will not tolerate gossip. He'd be content to sit in silence on a Saturday night rather than engage in a fun gabfest over drinks with my friends. Silence isn't my strongest skill—or contentment for that matter now that I think about it.

He doesn't even like to talk politics! How are we supposed to stay informed or figure out what we believe if we don't talk about it? I love that he loves hanging out with kids, and old people, and his friends, and random people we live next to. I'm just saying that if my life partner could bring himself to be a little chattier with me and my friends, maybe I'd feel more connected.

Even when he is home, I feel alone. Like last night. I had dished out a big bowl of chocolate chip cookie dough ice cream, sunk onto the sofa, wrapped myself in our fuzziest afghan, and prepared to enjoy the latest episode of *The Bachelor* with Eden and Andrew on speaker phone. I would have loved a warm husband to snuggle up against and trade caustic comments with. Instead, Josh wished me good night, kissed the top of my head, and climbed the stairs to our bedroom.

"Run, run for your life from that half-baked man-child!" Eden's disembodied voice warned the latest reality-show contestant searching for true love on national television. "Positive Attitude Coach is code for no job."

A lover of all the finer things in life, Eden is not only my friend and sometimes *Bachelor*-watching buddy, she's also my broker. When the twins first went to elementary school, I needed something flexible, so I got my realtor's license. For the first few years, I worked like a madwoman with something to prove. Come to think of it, maybe that was when Josh and I really started to drift apart. But now, I do the minimum to justify my expenses. Eden is fine either way. Whether we make money together or spend it, she's an equal fan of both. "Can you get me another glass of champagne, sweetheart?" I heard her ask Andrew. "I don't want to make Abby pause the rose ceremony."

Feeling a bit of a virtual third wheel, I begged off and watched the rest of the show by myself while scrolling through social media for scraps of human interaction and resenting that my husband would prefer to lay upstairs on our big king bed reading all alone than do something with me that I enjoy.

Josh would never forbid me from watching trashy TV, of course. He's not that kind of husband. But when I mentioned it was *Bachelor* night, his silence made it perfectly clear he wished I would choose different entertainment. Most of the time, I don't let his disapproval bother me. I work hard. I deserve to let my brain turn to mush for a few hours. It's harmless, victimless judgment when it's directed at people on TV. But this time… maybe I just imagined it, but as he turned away to climb the stairs, I thought I heard him sigh.

I don't need that guilt, so of course, I traded my bowl of ice cream for the rest of the carton.

When summer comes and I can't fit into my swimsuit, we will all know who's really to blame.

Dear Corel,

This is the real battlefield—not the bloody combat zone or the fight-to-the-finish epic struggles for which you are renowned. These ordinary everyday moments are where we fight for Abby's soul. She doesn't recognize her mind and heart as a battleground, and that is our enemy's greatest advantage. But you, as her Guardian, do.

She sees her vices as harmless little indulgences, but they are the foxes that ruin the vineyard. Our adversaries can use almost anything to drive a wedge between her and her husband. It doesn't matter if it's watching reality TV, shopping for the perfect curtains, or downing a few more glasses of wine. It's whatever she does to soothe and silence the true longing of her heart—whatever she does that distances herself from him.

Relationships are hard. Vulnerability is scary. But they are also life-giving and sanctifying. Humans long to be safe, seen, and soothed, as the psychiatrists say. Our Lord designed these needs to be met by healthy relationships and community. But our enemies have convinced her that sharing her needs will only bring pain—like the pain she felt when she asked her husband what he thought of all her work on his big surprise party.

To make our job even more difficult, they have also programmed her to interpret any pain or discomfort whatsoever as harm to be avoided instead of a gift. Pain is not only an important safeguard but often a necessary part of healing and growth.

They have lured her into thinking she will be safe and contented when she indulges in her little vices. She can get comfort from carbohydrates or thinks calorie counting will give her control. From her couch or her bed, she can feel the thrill of adventure, romance, competition, or lust through a screen, a book, or a device without any risk or damage. Or so she thinks. No addict—drug, sex, alcohol, social media or anything else—ever thought they'd be enslaved. But we know those seemingly little decisions add up, eroding her love, desensitizing her soul, and starving her of the connection she truly needs.

We need to help her see these lies for the intentionally created and nurtured deceptions that they are. Help her reframe her choices. Do you think she realizes she's choosing to watch TV, surf the web, and drink wine rather than regain the passion and love she once shared with her husband? Would she make a different choice if she knew what she was sacrificing? Let's help her to see the true cost of those choices she's been making.

Cheering for you, brave warrior, as you fight for the glory of Our Lord,

Ariam

Dear Stumbletrick,

The imagined sigh! Oh perfection—mine, not yours, of course. I'm drooling with delight at her animosity toward her husband for wanting to read a book. It seems my expert advice is finally penetrating that thick crusty skull of yours. I'm not sure who coined that phrase "comparison is the thief of joy," but you would do well to remember it and keep hammering that nail.

It appears you've stumbled into one of my favorite tricks. I like to call it the prison of comfort. It's elementary but effective—so perfect for you.

I will break it down into a simple analogy, so maybe even your rotting brain can grasp the objective and proceed accordingly.

Imagine the humans are locked in a debtor's prison. Our Enemy Above paid their debt, and if they simply realize this, they are free to go. So how do we keep them there?

Countless demons more talented than you have devoted whole fields of study to this dilemma, but I'll throw out a few options for illustration purposes.

You could try to convince them they *can't* get out—that once they are trapped, they will always be trapped, like the old circus trick of chaining baby elephants so that when they grow older they never try to break free.

Or you could try to frighten them with the possibilities of what lies outside their cell so that they prefer "the devil they know to the one they don't." Ha! That old adage holds more truth than they realize.

One of my favorites is to convince them to try to open the door with the wrong key (say, optimism or work ethic... or a happiness project) and watch as they struggle in frustration time and again to make it work. When

I use this technique, I also like to mock and shame them for their ineptitude while they struggle.

Those are all fine options, and there are many, many more, but you have unwittingly happened upon one of the best for American victims: Convince her that she doesn't want out.

I call it the prison of comfort. When Our Enemy Above tries to free her from the chains of her addictions and lead her to freedom, you should quietly ask her, "Does that make you happy?" or "Are you comfortable with that?"

If you doubt the power of something so simple or if it doesn't seem demonic enough, remember the Israelites and how they bemoaned giving up "garlics and leeks" for literal bread from Heaven and a daily divine pillar of fire leading them to the Promised Land. They didn't come to the conclusion that they'd be better off back in Egypt with taskmasters who had slaughtered their infant sons without a little demonic intervention. Impressive, but a little late to the tactic. If I had been in charge of that operation, they never would have left slavery in Egypt in the first place!

Got it? Simple enough for you? Now see if you can use that wart-covered noggin of yours to leverage this tool into tangible results.

Never let it be said that I don't give congratulations when due. In this case, the congratulations are due to myself, of course, for guiding you to your first modest success in this case. Don't get cocky about your small role—even a broken clock is right twice a day.

Time is ticking —

TwistTale

CHAPTER SIX

Victor

ABBY'S JOURNAL

Thursday, January 14th —

My therapist...I mean, life coach had me doing more walking down memory lane yesterday. This time she dredged up my life before Josh. Yuck.

I didn't tell her Lucas made a pass at me at the coffee shop because in truth, my relationship with him was a blip—not worth talking about, especially not when I'm paying for the conversation. He was just one of many of what I call Coke relationships—like when you have a Coke at a party after you've stopped drinking it regularly and wonder why you ever liked it in the first place. Maybe I do need to warn Jessica if they are still together after another couple of weeks, though.

I don't like thinking about him or really anything about my single years. They were so long ago. I like to think it's always been Josh and me together. When my life coach kept prying, I emphasized the glamorous side: Jessica and me out on the town—flirting, young, free, beautiful, bound only by our imaginations and our budget, pursuing our careers first and happy if we fell in love along the way because that seemed to be the acceptable order.

Back then, that was what I used to tell others, too. "Marriage? Maybe," I'd say to anyone who asked. "I want to explore, travel, create, study. If I find the right man, I might settle down, but looking at the options, I'm not holding my breath."

With my life coach, I opened my mouth to tell her the truth, but something stopped me. I don't feel safe anymore speaking my feelings if they contradict society's chosen narrative. There's no space to figure out things for ourselves. So I admit the truth only here in this journal where no one else will see.

What I remember most about being single was the sense of being alone, insecure, always outside, peeking through the windows of everyone else's lives—single in a coupled world. I'd go out with perfectly nice guys or narcissistic playboys but come home from both feeling emotionless and disillusioned. I wondered if I could ever fall in love or if I was permanently broken by all the disappointments. I wouldn't have called myself a man-hater—but I was heading down that path.

The worst part? I couldn't fix it on my own. As an independent problem solver, I hated to admit I wanted something I couldn't have. So, I didn't admit it. I resented the implication that my life was incomplete—possibly because I knew it was. Everyone acts like it's weak or "less than" to want to be a wife or a mother or even to have a long-term partner. But they also act like you must be broken if you are not or you don't. There's no winning.

It is not weak to want to be loved unconditionally, to be taken care of and to care for, to be kept safe and to keep safe. It's human. Or, maybe, we humans just don't want to admit that we need these things.

I can't explain or put my finger on it, but somehow along the way I realized I didn't like what was happening. I'm not strong enough to go against the tide all by myself. Ivy would decimate me with her feminist dogma, Eden would pity me, and Jessica has never been able to understand the concept of monogamy. But I know deep in my heart that I was sold a counterfeit.

The people my friends admired seemed to think there's more to life than romance, relationships, children, and families. We don't need husbands or children to be fulfilled, they'd say. But my affections told me otherwise. Why do so many of us pour over romance novels? How many books, songs, and movies are about love? How many ways can we write about it? An infinite number, apparently. We never seem to tire of it.

Marrying Josh wasn't a pleasant sidebar. It was a salve for an inescapable need. His unconditional love healed a gaping wound in my soul that my job, house, friends, and family could not. In truth, those were the things and people that helped inflict the wounds to begin with.

I don't want to hurt my single, divorced, or badly-married girlfriends. I know their pain, and I would never want to add to it, so I keep up the charade. Sure, in the beginning, I'd tell everyone who would listen how awesome Josh was, just like any newly-infatuated person would. But that's different from sharing the healing my marriage brought to deep wounds. I don't know how to talk about that without making them feel worse for not having it.

Maybe I'm a little parched now, but when I first got to know Josh, his love was like water to the desert of my thirsty soul.

He saw me. He didn't wait. He didn't flirt. He made no secret of his intentions. And I jumped at the chance to toss everything else away. My house, my nice car, my impressive job, even my friends and family—I would have traded them all for him—for this person who saw me and loved me best. I would be his delight, his favorite. Not for one night or a season, but forever. I know we pretend that life is about more than that, but I don't think it is. All the rest burns away like wood, hay, and stubble. God and people are all that's left. And the only thing really worth doing with people is loving them.

But believing that only brought me pain at their rejection.

Until Josh.

It wasn't love at first sight. Sure, he caught my fancy on the metro with the little boy, but that one "meet-cute" and dinner wasn't enough to restore hope in mankind or bring my broken heart back to life. My first inkling that this relationship and this person were truly different from anyone else I'd ever met came when he rescued me.

You never think of someone as a stalker. I met Victor long before Josh. Let me be clear—I never dated him. I only talked to him. He seemed harmless, interesting even, but that first conversation was enough to let him into my life, and then I couldn't get him out. A chance conversation turned into long emails, regular texts, then phone calls. Soon his ridiculously long messages began to seem manic instead of intriguing, his persistence invasive instead of flattering, and his talk of the future downright frightening. When he starting coming over to my house uninvited, I knew I had a problem.

Afraid to be at home alone, I started reaching out to other people, subtly, of course. *Maybe I could join you,* I suggested. *Maybe we could do dinner. Maybe you could come over.* I didn't want to beg. But no one—male or female, married or single—responded to my pleas. Perhaps they didn't see or hear my fear or desperation thinly veiled behind my casual words. Or perhaps they chose not to. I don't blame them. Everyone's busy with their own stuff.

But even though I had only just met Josh, he understood. He heard my cry for help.

Victor had transformed from a curiosity I was dabbling with to an annoyance I was trying to shed, but on this night, I realized he was beyond my control. He showed up uninvited, sat next to me on my couch, and talked about getting an apartment in the building next door! I remember watching his teeth as he droned on. He reminded me of a shark swirling around its prey. Calls and texts and public conversations were one thing, but never being able to get away from this large, overbearing, unwanted man even in my own home was another.

Desperate for him to leave, I tried all the social conventions—dropping hints, "It's getting late," crossing my arms, standing up. As he stood between me and the front door, I was doing everything I knew short of putting my hands flat against his chest and pushing him with all my force through the opening, so that I could slam the door shut behind him and slide the deadbolt into place.

But I didn't even try. Looking up at him, dwarfed by his seventy-pound weight advantage, for the first time, I realized with crystal clarity that I *couldn't* force him to go. Kind of like I couldn't stop him from wrapping his sweaty arms around me and pulling me against his protruding belly. I think he even pressed his lips and beard against the top of my head.

And then, mercifully he left.

But I was scared. I didn't want to be alone in the house, so I texted Josh, "Can you come over tonight?"

"On my way."

I didn't know then that he left a meeting, bolted out the door, and fought an hour of traffic to get to me.

He wrapped his arms around me as soon as he saw me. "You okay?"

"Of course!" I laughed, pretending he had misread the seriousness of my appeal, but I couldn't have been more relieved—or impressed—if he had ridden up on a white charger wearing a suit of armor.

We didn't talk about Victor. Well, not really. I joked about it, dropping breadcrumbs in my conversations, hoping he would notice and care enough to follow. "I think I might have a stalker," I said with feigned excitement as if I had announced I had a new puppy. Josh let his draped arm on the back of the sofa fall onto my shoulders and gave me a small squeeze.

He didn't ask me to explain or defend myself. *What are you talking about? Did you lead him on? Why did you let him in?* Nope. Josh was just there for me—and relief flooded my body. I allowed my head to drop onto his shoulder. He ordered take out, and we ate fish tacos, drank margaritas, and chatted for hours. Our conversation stayed light. Although we did joke about using code words in case my stalker came over again. "If you text 'rescue,' I'll call. Put me on speaker and I'll ask why you're so late for our appointment," he suggested. "Or if you'd rather, text 'help' and I'll send a SWAT team."

I didn't want him to go. I loved that feeling of safety—being so close beside him, feeling his presence, understanding, warmth, and protection. I don't know the last time we sat together like that for hours. I'm sure it's been years. I wouldn't even know how to anymore. I would feel silly trying.

Friday, January 15th —

So yet another attempt at the happiness commandments tonight (#2 act the way I want to feel and #4 connect meaningfully with others), this time with Jessica as I feel like my efforts with Lucas, Ivy, and Eden were all a bit of a strike out.

But our conversation took a weird turn.

I had invited her over for a *Bridgerton* marathon, one of the few shows we both like. She loves the "yummy soft porn," and I love British accents, costumes, and scenery. We hadn't seen each other since Josh's party, so we had a lot to catch up on over the charcuterie board and wine—including laughing about my new life coach dredging up the old memories I hate (commandment #2).

"Whatever happened with that stalker guy?" she asked between popping chocolate-covered almonds in her mouth, her legs curled up under her on the sofa.

"Victor? Oh, I don't know. I told him I wasn't comfortable seeing or talking to him anymore. Eventually, he stopped reaching out."

"No, I mean between him and Josh," she clarified.

"What are you talking about? There wasn't anything between Victor and Josh."

"You don't know?" She raised her eyebrows at me over her glass.

"Know what?"

"Josh confronted Victor the night you told him you had a stalker." Now it was my turn to be surprised. Josh had never mentioned anything about that.

"He told my boyfriend at the time in case Victor didn't stop bothering you," she continued. "I guess he figured having a lawyer involved couldn't hurt. I thought he'd have told you. Most guys want their girlfriends to know when they chase away the bad guys."

"I thought my standing up to him convinced him to go away."

"You're so naïve, Abby." Jessica laughed. "Guys like that don't go away on their own. When you start to resist, that's when they dig in. It makes them feel powerful, exerting their will against yours. Men like Victor don't have a lot of power, so they take it where they can get it."

Huh. It seemed like Josh rescued me more than I knew. But that was a long time ago. Now he doesn't seem to care who I hang out with. I thought he'd be upset when Lucas showed up at his birthday party, but he never said a word about that. I could have an affair, and he probably wouldn't even notice.

CHAPTER SEVEN

Subterfuge

Stumbletrick,

For Hell's sake, you are dead wrong on this affair thing. How many times do I have to tell you? You don't know your spiky tail from your mucus-crusted nose on this continent.

But blaming *me* for *your* ineptitude takes the cake. I do have other responsibilities than leading you around by the nose. Not that it's any of your business, but I've been spearheading some really impressive work in psychotropic drugs, negative polarization, sex-positivity, and persuasive design, just to name a few. Like all my fancy words? Subterfuge, baby! This is what I'm trying to teach you.

You Eastern simpletons slather at the piles of bloody corpses after a mass shooting, but masterminds like me keep 'em coming. The human vermin cry over the bodies of children, but thanks to my skills they can't even figure out where to focus their rage. *It's the guns! It's the drugs! It's the lack of drugs! It's the video games! It's the hateful speech! It's the lack of speaking hatefully enough.* And then there's my favorite—*If you're silent, you're complicit!*

It's delicious. That's what it is, Stumbletrick. Brilliant. In fact, the word *masterpiece* might be in order. Definitely some of my better work. Put simply, create the fog of war. Your enemy can't fight back if they don't know where to aim. If they try, they'll most likely take out a few allies in the attempt. That's what it's all about on this continent—blurred lines. I've got them so twisted up, most young people today don't even have the *capacity* to make moral judgements, let alone the will power. Nothing is Good or True—it's just your preference or opinion. Stop them from naming evil and good long enough and soon they can't even to tell the difference.

But enough about my brilliance. Let's focus on your lack thereof. I have let you flounder long enough. The powers that be have noticed your pathetic performance, and I can't have it reflecting poorly on my mentorship. Thus, as of now I'll be taking a more active role in your victim's corruption.

First, ditch the life coach. Introspection is dangerous. Your victim wouldn't normally be dwelling on the past like she has been because, for years, I've kept her and the rest of America preoccupied. Control their thoughts and the body will follow (and eventually their souls). What your client needs is subtle distraction, not in-your-face adultery.

Second, convince her she needs a new house.

Before you start complaining that wanting a new house is not even sinful, I'm telling you now, I don't want to hear it. I don't need to justify my methods to you. Just do it. Don't despise small beginnings. A game of chess isn't lost in the last move. It's lost when your opponent decides to trade a pawn for a knight without realizing what that swap will cost four moves later. A cleverer demon would recognize this fantastic opportunity—more than you deserve—to glimpse behind the curtain at the machinations of a master deceiver. Let's see if you can manage for once to follow a simple command of your superior without question.

Plant in her mind the burning conviction that a physical possession will meet all her deepest needs and desires. In your victim's case, it needs to be something significant. If we were to convince her she merely needed the latest electronic gadget, she could simply go out, procure it, and the ruse would be up. While an affair would definitely distract her from her husband, the desire for a house distracts *and* allows us to fly under her moral radar.

I'll share a powerful word with you—aspirational. Sounds so much nicer than greed and infinitely better than that old-fashioned notion of covetousness, right? Americans don't covet. They passed right by it, along with greed and envy, a long time ago. They *aspire*. They have #goals. Rather than longing to possess an item in an ad, they aspire to have the *life* portrayed in the ad. A single possession will never do it. They chase a dream they cannot achieve while failing to understand it's the wrong dream anyway. Delicious.

Practically speaking, since you seem to require hand-holding, the next time she encounters a problem—big or small—suggest a new house as the solution. The kids are arguing. "If only both of them could have their own space when they come home." She and her husband don't spend time together. "If we lived closer to his work, he wouldn't have such a long commute." She has no real friends. "If we had a bigger dining room, we could invite people over." She's lazy. "If we moved, I could finally get organized and not be overwhelmed by all this clutter." You get the picture.

Just plant the thoughts like I'm telling you. Then, watch and learn.

It's not that hard. Don't screw this up —

Twisttale

ABBY'S JOURNAL

Saturday, January 16th —

It's a little scary how our cell phones have taken over our lives. Apparently, they listen even when we're not using them. I merely mentioned to Eden how beautiful those new houses on Regency Row are, and now Zillow ads are popping up all over my Facebook feed. I know we can't afford to move, and I don't have any clients currently looking in that area, but visiting a few open houses would be fun. Market research, you know.

Sunday, January 17th —

Ooh, I feel like I'm making great progress on my happiness project this weekend! #1 I'm keeping up with my journaling every day (paying attention to what I'm paying attention to, mainly Josh not wanting to hang out with me). #2 I'm acting the way I want to feel—confident, successful, forward-thinking. I even made up a whole backstory for the selling agents about my newly empty-nester, cash-paying buyers. And #3 I remembered something that brings me joy—house hunting! It's so much better than social media. No one shames me. No one makes me feel bad. I just look at gorgeous homes and dream about what my life could be like. And I don't have to deal with unrealistic expectations from picky clients. This new hobby seems to push all the right buttons.

Who knows? Maybe I'll even find an amazing deal we could afford, and I could do my own extreme home makeover, just like Joanna Gaines. Surfing Zillow and the MLS is better than bingeing on Netflix, right?

Tuesday, January 19th —

Josh isn't encouraging my new habit. He won't go to open houses or even look at listings with me. Big surprise: once again he doesn't like to do the things I do.

When I suggested he come downstairs and watch House Hunters, he suggested I come up to the bedroom with him instead. "We don't need a new house, Abby," he argued. "I hardly see you in this one." He added that with a wink. Seriously? He doesn't do what I want, but then expects me to do what he wants?

But that's okay. That's what I have girlfriends for. Commandment #4, right? Connect meaningfully with others. Eden is more than thrilled to go to the open houses with me when she can squeeze it into her busy schedule. She does have champagne taste, though, turning up her nose at all the fixer-uppers. She's taken to sending me links to the most gorgeous kitchens, bathrooms, and closets. Oh, the closets! With plush rugs, miniature benches, and drawers full of color-coordinated clothes folded Marie Kondo-style. Talk about sparking joy! Who wouldn't have a smile on her face each morning if she got to start the day admiring rows of shoes and purses neatly arranged on shelves instead of digging through piles?

"Where would we put my clothes?" Josh asked when I showed him an inspiration pic.

"Oh, I'm just dreaming, honey," I assured him.

"And your dreams don't account for me anymore?" He was joking. I think.

I smiled but avoided his gaze.

I hadn't realized until he said it, but no, my dreams haven't included him for a long time.

Wednesday, January 20th —

A house listing caught my eye today and stopped me in my tracks. Like someone had conjured an image straight from my brain, the cover photo was exactly what I had imagined as the perfect home when Josh and I were engaged. Back then, I daydreamed about one of those historic Greek revivals with towering shade trees, gracious white columns, expansive green lawn, and hilltop views. Now my tastes have matured, and that style seems a little old fashioned. Of course, when we were starting out, we couldn't afford a house like that, but I had sure wanted one. No modern trends, metal, glass, or steel for me. I wanted classic beauty.

Maybe it's because I came from nothing. I brag now about my pioneer roots like they're a badge of honor, but the truth is there are lots of dark places in my past that are nothing to be proud of. When you come from old money like Josh does, you take your place in the world for granted. I didn't. I scrapped and fought to get where I was, and I wanted to at least *look* like I belonged. Josh didn't care that much about sidewalk appeal. He was more interested in space for having friends over for dinner. And oh my goodness, he loved spending time out on our front porch talking with the neighbors, his friends, or whoever might pass by.

I don't care as much about looking like I belong any more. I *know* I belong after years of hard work. At the moment, I'm more concerned about others coming along and taking what we've got.

Back to this house listing, I literally gasped when I saw it. It's way too big and expensive for us, but it reminded me of my old dreams. It's so lovely, and it's located right by Josh's parents. It doesn't hurt to look at beautiful things, right? In fact, I think it helps—healthier than drudging up all those painful memories with my life coach. Remembering the happiness we had only makes the present state more painful. I think I'll skip therapy, I mean my life coaching session, this week and look at more houses.

Dear Corel,

Nice pivot. Not only did you identify the movement of the enemy—which is more than half the battle—but you used a glimpse of that house to turn her attention back to her first love. Well done.

Kudos to you for recognizing the suddenness of Abby's new preoccupation as a sign of our enemy's handiwork instead of simply her natural craving for beauty, truth, and goodness. Tiny seeds of discontentment, bitterness, and resentment about any matter big or small can cause inestimable damage when they remain in the dark. When hidden and nurtured, these seemingly insignificant thoughts can spread into a network of roots so invasive that trying to remove them would almost tear her heart apart. We must identify and expose them for the ugly weeds they are before we can tame and destroy them.

By the way, we aren't actually bothered by whether she gets a new house or not. Our Lord is not more glorified when His children live in austerity than when they live in abundance. He cares about the condition of Abby's heart, not the size of her home.

But our enemy is shrewd, and he has planted these seeds of discontentment for a reason. He knows Americans tend to substitute possessions for relationships and square footage for friends. Should we sit back and watch until we figure out his larger plan, or work to undo their every action knowing each is intended for her harm?

I eagerly await your input. I know Our Lord chose you for this assignment for a reason. You are doing great.

For His Glory,

Ariam

Stumbletrick,

Have you even been to battle? Is corruption so easy in the East and the demonic hold on humans so powerful that you use only one technique at a time?

You don't send a single arrow to skewer your victim's heart. You send a volley, then charge with horsemen while arrows rain from the sky. You scale the side walls while they are distracted by the frontal assault. Swoop around and encircle or divide them, so they must fight on multiple fronts. It's called war, you idiot.

I thought I'd seen the height of your imbecility until you wrote, "I thought we were supposed to be making her comfortable, but now we're making her discontent?" Yes! Make her comfortable in her spiritual poverty and discontent with her material wealth. Try to keep up.

Then, along with your stupid, disrespectful questions, you also glossed over critical intel like her addiction to her iPhone, Facebook, and other social media. What is it going to take for you to grasp the superiority of subtlety?

Her irresistible desire for constant distraction and instant gratification is precisely the sort of clandestine bondage I've been talking about. I am flabbergasted by your failure to capitalize on it. Instead, you continue to harp about more traditional temptations—as if co-opting your victim's time, attention, and emotions during most of her waking hours somehow ranks as a consolation prize.

Combine her social media addiction with our hold over her eating and sleeping habits, and we could have her almost entirely in our control! Our grip would be secure even if she was absorbing content as innocuous as gardening tips—though we know that the vast majority of social media is quite anti-social, to put it mildly.

Here in America, we demons embrace technology. Work smarter, not harder, as they say. In the past, we took great pains to nurture the shame narrative in our victim's minds. We had to. We had to counteract our Divine Adversary's blasphemous depiction of them as His beloved lost children, so valuable that He would literally sacrifice His own son to be reconciled with them.

We would murmur "you are pathetic" at just the moment when they stumbled. We would sigh "you are hopeless" when they tried again. And finally, we would whisper "you are a fraud" when they sought to put on a brave face.

Now, we no longer have to whisper. We simply direct them to their phones or computer screens. In the virtual world, our message of shame screams from every corner. Every airbrushed photo helps convince her she is not beautiful. Every vitriol-filled comment reinforces that she is worthy of a full arsenal of hate and loathing if she does not repeat verbatim the party line or signal the right set of virtues. Every list of must-haves, must-dos, or must-not-says reminds her "you are not enough."

And that's just the adults. The potential damage of unrestrained ridicule of vulnerable adolescents via cyberspace makes my head spin. I can almost taste all those juicy hell-bound souls. They have hundreds of disparaging voices whispering in their ears. With all these humans doing our work for us, we almost don't even need to add our own. The recent sky-rocketing suicide rate bears witness to what fruit these "small" temptations eventually yield.

This, Stumbletrick, is pure gold. Dig in. Feed her addiction to that dopamine fix when someone likes her posts. Keep her scrolling, scrolling, scrolling, always searching for more. Focus her attention on that tiny screen ignoring the beauty of the world and the people around her. Like Pavlov's dogs who salivated at the mere sound of a bell, make the buzz of her phone irresistible to ignore. The content is irrelevant—the IKEA catalog, *Bachelor* gossip, new house listings, or *Fifty Shades of Grey.* Like the lead pipe, rope, or revolver, any will work. Use whichever is handiest. It doesn't matter which.

Humans do not realize they are enslaved and formed by their habits. They imagine their routines to be as fragile as spiderwebs—easily broken and recreated. But each repetition deepens the grooves in their brain's neuropathways. Every time they reach for their phone, their drink, that next bite, the remote control—whatever fix they use to soothe the pain and isolation—twists another strand around their will until they hang, trapped and powerless as an insect waiting to be devoured.

Smartphones have made our roles easier. No need for you to think up new ways to lure her away from spending time with the Divine Adversary or doing His work each day. Just continue to cultivate this addiction and your work is done for you. She will wake up each morning to the siren call of her phone, turn to it instinctively in each free moment throughout the day, and regretfully lay it aside each night until her life is spent. We will then finally devour her soul and gnaw on her bare bones.

I salivate just thinking about it—

Twisttale

CHAPTER EIGHT
Operation Heritage

ABBY'S JOURNAL

Friday, January 22nd —

Despite what Ruthie says, I'm *not* obsessed with house hunting. I'm just enthusiastic and passionate, and I have a bit of an addictive personality. I can't help it. But it does have benefits as well as liabilities. I'd love to channel it into something healthy like eating more fruits and vegetables or being a gym rat like Jessica, but those streaks never last long.

More often, I hop from Netflix bingeing to house renovating to Facebook scrolling to finishing off a half-gallon of ice cream alone in the pantry. At least I'm aware of my weaknesses. That's something.

Plus, house hunting doesn't hurt anyone. I don't think anyone ever lost friends or couldn't fit into their clothes from surfing MLS or Zillow late into the night or attending too many open houses.

So Ruthie can mind her own business. She's been rolling her eyes and mouthier than usual. Maybe she's afraid a new house might mean we'd find a new person to help out or we wouldn't need her anymore. But if I weren't analyzing maps or sketching renovation plans, I know she'd be judging me for whatever else I was doing. At least this is harmless.

What isn't harmless are her comments to the twins when they were home over winter break. I can't believe she told Destiny she wasn't proud of being an American, and she flat out discouraged Cash from applying for that ROTC scholarship.

Of course, Ruthie's entitled to her own opinion about America, but what really upset me was Josh's reaction. Instead of politely ignoring and then disregarding what she said, he encouraged her to elaborate—affirming her views right in front of the kids! We don't have that much time with them anymore, and they are already getting enough new-fangled ideas at school without the two of them piling on.

It's always bothered me that Josh is not more patriotic. My dad was in the military. He taught me to show respect for the American flag and to stand and put my hand over my heart when the national anthem is played. I always thought I would marry someone more clean-cut like Tom Cruise in *Top Gun* and less bearded Middle Easterner with long hair.

But having lived in various places, Josh's family is more cosmopolitan and didn't teach him patriotism. It's not like he doesn't love America. He just doesn't think it's that important. He doesn't have Lee Greenwood's voice in his head like I do, and I'm not even sure he's seen a John Wayne movie.

That's usually fine. I take the lead in passing love of country on to our kids since I care about it more. But when Josh gives Ruthie a platform by saying things like "Tell me more about why you feel that way," it makes it harder for me to teach the kids our values. I don't want to seem as if I disagree with him, but a lot of people sacrificed and died to give us the freedoms we enjoy as Americans, and if we don't teach our children to fight for those freedoms, they will disappear.

I tried to talk to him about it, but he laughed and said, "So it would make you feel better if the kids and I watch *True Grit?*" When I pressed, he gave me of the old "give unto Caesar the things that are Caesar's" line. Like that even applies in this case. He refuses to see it my way and said, "Don't you think we should focus more on what America can become than try to hold onto what it has been?" Why do I even try? We aren't going see eye-to-eye, which is fine I guess, as long as he doesn't undermine me. If the idea wasn't so ridiculous, I'd think he and Ruthie were teaming up against me.

Stumbletrick,

Shut. Your. Mouth. I can't take another word of your infuriating arrogance and disrespect. I don't owe you an explanation, but I can't take another minute of your moronic rantings.

Boring, Stumbletrick? You think suburban American women are *boring*? Breaking up a marriage and fanning the flames of discontentment and greed aren't as glamorous as your previous escapades? I'm afraid low-hanging fruit like jihad and genocide have given demons like you false confidence about your skills.

I'm not sure I can help someone who prefers Kool-Aid to Cabernet. Machine guns and machetes may cause pain and division, but bringing down souls without detection takes skill and finesse. Their souls, not their bodies, are our ultimate prey, after all.

Sit back on your haunches for a few minutes. We're going to have a history lesson. Even if you are transferred soon as I have recommended, technology is bringing humans closer together. We wouldn't want demonic labor on one side of the globe to sabotage efforts on the other.

Here in America, we have been perfecting and tweaking our demonic infrastructure for centuries with great success, although those successes might not be as apparent to the unsophisticated observer—or demons with lower security clearance. The last thing we need is for an ambitious, know-it-all, glory-hungry upstart to inadvertently punch a hole in the delicate facade of American Christianity because he doesn't understand it. The landscape you underestimate is the result of more than two centuries of careful cultivation of nominal Christian followers whose practice is more culture and habit than devotion and faith.

But I'm getting ahead of myself. Take a look at Plymouth. I and the other demons on this continent took the unwavering faith of an irritatingly devout little ragtag bunch of pilgrims and, within a mere fifty years (a single generation!), had their children at war with the children of the very humans who saved them from starvation, all the while believing themselves to be doing the work of our Divine Adversary. That, my friend, requires a special level of expertise.

We didn't invent self-righteousness in America. The demons working with the Jewish Pharisees lay claim to that. But I'd say we perfected this ultimate weapon against religious people. And boy, those Pilgrims, Puritans, and Founding Fathers were serious about their religion. The desire to worship according to their conscience, as well as their revulsion at European excess and corruption, fueled the entire enterprise. We would have been fools to try to lure them out of such deeply entrenched, heavily-defended territory with conventional temptations.

They locked down in tight communities and committed to the study of the Bible, regular self-examination (even the most liberal of the founding fathers, that philanderer Franklin, was famous for his gargantuan efforts on that score), fervent prayer, loyal church attendance, and a strictly-enforced moral code. To get around such strong defenses, we had to discover the chink in their armor.

Sure, we could always lure away a few errant souls with individual temptations. There's a reason the Puritans needed those scarlet A's. But those are small potatoes compared to the damage that can be inflicted by perpetuating a whole culture based on a false premise. For every wayward soul caught in a single act of fornication, we convinced hundreds that a lifetime of condemnation, judgment, and self-righteousness actually made them holier. Then, as all sins do when allowed to grow and flourish unchecked, their spiritual pride bore fruit for us.

You might not realize it now because we have so thoroughly neutralized it, but America posed a significant threat to us at one time. Our Divine

Adversary had such an unfair advantage. All he needs is a small group of truly devout humans. Remember those twelve pathetic fishermen, tax collectors, and other miscreants? They are proof that with sincere faith from even a few imbeciles, He can wreck the work of a million demons.

Imagine an entire nation founded by and largely populated with humans devoted to Him. That was the very real possibility we were facing. Worse, not content to merely have the freedom to worship and follow their own consciences, they were explicit in their desire to actively use America as a base to spread Christianity and its political freedom to the rest of the world!

I'm not at liberty to divulge the highly-classified specific tactics to anyone without proper clearance. Discretion is paramount in deception operations. But you don't have to be a genius to see the results. Just open those beady red eyes of yours a little wider.

Surely you can see the legalism, greed, and racism we slid into their original sincere desire to spread their faith, perverting it with notions of racial superiority—quite a natural complement to that spiritual pride we discussed.

Like the proverbial frog in the frying pan, we gradually turned up the heat until those one-time pious believers and their Christian nation were annihilating one race and enslaving another in the process of fulfilling their so-called Manifest Destiny. We have been so skillful that they are only starting to see through the ruse now, hundreds of years in.

As you can see, America is not boring. The weapons we use in the Western hemisphere are no less powerful, and the pain we inflict no less excruciating, than those used by the demons in the Eastern hemisphere. I would argue they are often more so. I'd put the pain, torment, hatred, and all the rest caused by the treatment of Blacks and Natives in America up against any other accomplishment we demons have ever achieved. We're still reaping the benefits.

And this suffering was often inflicted by scripture-quoting, church-attending, public-prayer-writing humans who honestly believed they were doing their Father's work. They bought and sold other humans, treated them as chattel, and systematically removed, oppressed, or killed an entire race so that they could prosper from their land. Do you need any more evidence of how powerful a weapon these subtle but pervasive lies can be?

In America, we wield tools of torture with a surgeon's skill rather than a soldier's bravado. Our strategy depends on lulling the humans into complacency while tightening the cords, creating a culture that binds them in our trap before we begin our torment in earnest in eternity.

You lack perspective, Stumbletrick. Yes, it's fun to watch the humans bleed, but think of our methods as more akin to the relentless drip of Chinese water torture than a few violent minutes of waterboarding. Think about that and decide which is really more delicious.

One more thing about this little lesson. It's not really history. You're about to watch these long-simmering lies explode all over that "boring" American suburban life.

Next time you disrespect me and my work, you won't just get a tongue lashing.

I'll rip out your tongue once and for all—

Twisttale

Dear Corel,

You ask such great questions. I always enjoy hearing your input, and I certainly understand why you would be confused. Why does Abby care if Ruthie isn't proud to be an American, or if her son joins the military, or if Josh likes John Wayne? I know it seems foreign to you that patriotism is so important to Abby. I'll try to explain.

You see, America is a special place. Its origin wasn't like that of other countries—driven by territorial or genealogical disputes. Its founders weren't perfect by any means, but they were different in that they were motivated by ideas, specifically the concepts of liberty, equality, and self-government. These were new at the time—that people could govern themselves and not need a king, or a chief, or an emperor with an army to make and enforce laws. Western writers started to opine about humans having equal dignity and being free to do what is right. Of course, the American founders didn't execute these ideas perfectly. Some restricted them to their own race or gender, but they created a foundation for a freer society than any humans had known before or since.

So what does that have to do with Josh, or Abby, or Ruthie? Well, that's where it gets complicated. Remember, our enemy plants his most poisonous thorns deep inside beautiful facades.

America is beautiful. Abby rightfully admires the nobility of people who pledged their lives, fortunes, and sacred honor to fight for their freedom and the freedom of others. She respects the courage and sacrifice of the untold millions since then who have died in defense of that idea. But as they often do, our adversaries have twisted something true, good, and noble and used it for their own purposes.

That French philosopher Voltaire (and more recently, Abby's muse Gretchen Rubin) got it backwards. "The perfect is the enemy of the good" may apply if you're trying to finish a novel. But like so many human philosophies, the Kingdom of God turns that notion on its head. The great deceiver twists the good of America into the enemy of the perfection to which Our Lord calls His followers. Being a good citizen isn't the point. He is holy and perfect and desires for them to be the same as well. American civic pride may not be the worst thing, but virtuous humility is better. And in the hands of our enemies, pride—even pride in something good and beautiful—can be a powerful weapon for destruction of souls.

More than ever she needs you at her side—to light and guard, rule and guide as the prayer goes.

Keep guiding her toward the Very Best,

Ariam

ABBY'S JOURNAL

Saturday, January 23rd —

Since talking to Josh didn't seem to get me anywhere, I went directly to Ruthie.

In retrospect, that might have been a mistake.

"Ruthie, I want to talk to you about something." I pulled up a barstool at the kitchen island.

"You know those things you said to the kids about not loving or being proud of our country? Please don't make comments like that."

She stopped humming mid-verse. Uh oh.

Ruthie—strong, dark, whip-smart, and sharp-tongued—had been helping us around the house since the twins were babies. I couldn't have gotten by without her back then, but if I'm honest, I'll admit I've also always been a little afraid of her. I'm not sure why, but maybe it's because I never know for sure how she might react. Kind of like right now.

She swiveled to face me, the pan she had been washing still in her hand, "So now you're going to try to tell me what I can and can't say?"

"Of course, you can say whatever you like on your own time, but when the kids are here, yes, there are some things we'd rather you not discuss with them." I tried to keep my voice steady.

"We? Josh didn't seem to mind." Ruthie began washing the dish again.

Breathe, I reminded myself as I clenched my teeth and tried to control my irritation. I closed my eyes for a moment, took a breath, and then continued, "This isn't Nazi Germany. You can say what you want, but I don't think you will like the consequences." I didn't mean to sound ominous. It just sort of slipped out in my effort to appear firm.

Ruthie took a full five seconds to dry her hands on her apron before she turned, set them on her wide hips, and asked, "Is that a threat?" Great. Now, I've poked the bear, just what I was trying to avoid. I don't know why I let her intimidate me. This is my house, and I'm perfectly within my rights to make the rules. It's her job to follow them. I could feel the anger welling up inside of me.

"It's a fact—you reap what you sow." My tone was sharper than I intended. "It's the way the world works. I hope we're clear." I started for the door as I didn't want a long conversation. But I'm willing to bet I'm going to be hearing more, not fewer, irritating comments from Ruthie from now on. She doesn't make anything easy.

Stumbletrick,

Stop. Just stop. You have no idea what you are talking about. Delving into American politics is way above your pay grade. You should have been able to execute the mission without kicking over this can of worms. But you've taken a straightforward task and somehow managed to threaten an entire operation.

According to our superiors, who obviously don't know you, I have no choice but to bring you in under the tent. Destroy this letter after you read it. Secrecy is critical. First rule of Operation Heritage is that we don't talk about Operation Heritage.

Remember, your access is on a need-to-know basis. The details of this clandestine campaign, which, yes, I did mastermind, will remain top secret. This missive will divulge only what you need to know to complete your assignment without further damaging our larger operation.

Dig deep into that crusty head of yours and see if you can remember your education in denial and deception tactics, things like Operation Fortitude when the Allies tricked Hitler with phantom field armies threatening attack in the north and south to divert his attention from the impending D-Day attack on Normandy. The most effective deception operations are incredibly complex and coordinated, and a single intelligence slip-up can jeopardize the entire plan. Unfortunately, some of our most senior demons fail to recognize the brilliance and complexity of my work and allow numbskulls like you to come over and gum up the works.

During your time on this continent, you have observed some of your victim's idiosyncrasies when it comes to American government. Until now, I've ignored your comments and questions, like wondering why her church honors members of their armed forces and sings their national anthem during church services or why she talks to her kids more about

George Washington and Thomas Jefferson than Saint Augustine or even Martin Luther. But your ignorance now threatens one of our most successful deceptions.

I will try to use small words. Humans were created to worship. It's in their DNA. The first two commandments Our Enemy gave the vermin were about idolatry—have no other gods before him and don't make, serve, or bow down to idols. Yet our victim skips right by those two commandments, confident they don't apply to her because she doesn't have a Buddhist shrine in her living room.

We gave her a false god. We told her America is a Christian nation, that patriotism equates with godliness. We convinced her that loving and serving her country is synonymous with loving and serving her Creator. Brilliant, right? Because it came from me. Of course, she doesn't know we intentionally fed her that lie. It's buried so deep in her psyche that she doesn't suspect a thing. If she did, the gig would be up—which is why we don't want her ruminating on the fact Josh is not particularly patriotic.

You see how quickly she abandons the admonitions to love her neighbor, let alone her enemies, when they so much as support an opposing political candidate? That's the kind of fruit you are jeopardizing fanning this particular conflict. I want you (not her) to notice how she reserves her most intense anger, not for fellow Christians being tortured in the Middle East or slaughtered in Africa, not for churches blown up in China or burned down in India, but instead for political comments on social media she doesn't approve of. You can't get those results with run-of-the-mill, garden-variety temptation.

In a way, I'm glad you stumbled into this because it truly is one of my most ingenious plans in this country, which is saying something. That's one of the drawbacks of cloak-and-dagger work—no accolades. This is not a learn-by-example opportunity, though. It would take years to untangle and dissect the deep roots of this deception. All you need to know at this point is that we are currently reaping the hard-won fruit that I planted long ago, so back off and let it be.

This letter won't destroy itself, so be sure you do after reading it. And remember, if you let the name of this operation pass through your rotting teeth, I'll make sure it's the last thing you let slip.

Choke one more time and I'll choke you—

Twisttale

Dear Faithful Warrior,

I know it's hard to be away from the Heavenly realm. It takes intestinal fortitude to stomach Abby's grossly distorted view of reality day-in and day-out, especially without being able to refresh yourself with Our Lord's presence and worshiping around His throne. I respect and admire your devotion to duty, though, in refusing to leave our girl's side. Take comfort in knowing that you are not alone—your name and Abby's are frequently on our lips and in our hearts as our prayers and those of the saints waft up to the court of the Lord.

Courage and patience, dear Corel. And baby steps. She didn't get here overnight after all but from decades of intentional deception by our enemy and willful disobedience of her own. Of course, we know our Lord can do anything, but more often we see Him shaping humans with the practiced, patient hand of a master potter rather than the oft-prayed for Road-to-Damascus-style instant transformation.

The good news is you have much to work with. Truth is all around her. His message of truth will resonate in her soul if we can find a way to break through the noise. Who could hear anything at all with all those voices competing for her attention?

Try whispering in the still of the night or those first waking hours of the morning. Humans are more open and receptive to the stirrings of their hearts when they've had a few hours of quiet stillness. I've heard other angels have had success when their charges are walking or even driving. If you can't persuade her to be away from the distraction of her phone for a mere hour, try hiding her earbuds.

Lift her eyes to the sky—every moment is a masterpiece of light and color. The Great Creator has illustrated His truth throughout His creation. Perhaps you could turn her gaze to an eagle soaring or ants laboring. Or have her notice spiders weaving webs like those entangling her to help her understand her own situation better. Even the plants and how they grow and thrive contain spiritual truths. One can see His fingerprints everywhere. Like, for instance, *their* fingerprints. Do you know that He created every single human unique? No face is the same, each a separate work of art, yet all with that same flicker of His divine light inside—made in His image. Amazing!

I wonder if Abby has ever noticed how beautiful Ruthie is? Does she only hear the impudence but not her boldness and unfailing confidence? Is her ear attuned first and foremost to hear mocking rather than wisdom, truth, or beauty from Ruthie's lovely voice? Does she see God's provision in Ruthie's strength and skill or does she only calculate wages paid versus services rendered?

Abby wasn't always this way, you know. Our dear beautiful girl, beloved daughter, has forgotten who she was created to be—and who the others around her are. But Our Lord has not forgotten. He has sent us to rescue her, but the strands that bind are strong, the deception thick.

He will show us how.

I know it doesn't sound very angelic, but sometimes the first step is discontentment in a relationship. She has to want to change. She needs to feel something is missing. She needs to realize that something's not right. As long as she's comfortable, she's secure in the grasp of lies.

Keep gently trying to stir up the ache in her heart, but if it doesn't work, we'll have to resort to more aggressive measures.

For the Glory of Our Lord,

Ariam

ABBY'S JOURNAL

Sunday, January 24th —

New day. Fresh start. I'm going to forget about my frustration with Ruthie and Josh and re-focus back on my happiness project. What did my life coach say? I can't change other people, only myself. So, what are some concrete steps (other than my house shopping habit) I can take to make progress on my happiness commandments?

Let's see, *Pay more attention to what I pay attention to.* Maybe I should start a gratitude journal.

Act the way I want to feel. Exercise?

Connect meaningfully with others. Start a blog?

Okay, all too ambitious. I need baby steps. My life coach also said creating micro-habits will supposedly set me up for success.

Remember things that bring me joy.

I'll do that one. I'll focus on the positive posts on Facebook that bring me joy instead of the ones that enrage me. I'll read some of those sugary sweet, this-will-put-a-smile-on-your-face sort of posts and scroll past the infuriating ones I naturally gravitate toward. And I'll download a motivational self-help book to listen to while I'm driving around or sitting in traffic because feeling productive brings me joy. Okay, I'm getting excited. I can do these things. I don't need to define myself by what my husband might think of me. I am my own person.

Yay me! I've got this! (*Acting the way I want to feel*, right there, and I'm connecting meaningfully with others by taking Jess as my guest at the broker open houses this afternoon.)

CHAPTER NINE

Jessica

Stumbletrick,

You are truly an imbecile. I let you in under the tent on pure tactical gold like Operation Heritage, and you come back with concerns about insignificant inspirational drivel.

You seriously think I would care about a stupid letter floating over social media from a non-existent daughter to an imaginary mother? *"Dear Mom, you are enough. You don't have to be the perfect mom, or prettier, or stronger, ... I see you beating yourself up. You think you have to do it all...."*

Blah blah blah. Gag.

How many daughters have ever said such a thing to a mother? They are more likely to say, "I see you surfing on your phone during my performance, hiding from me in the pantry eating my Halloween candy, and locking yourself in the bathroom with a bottle of wine." She isn't enough. That's the truth. She can never be enough! Who do they think they are? Sure, we like to torture them by pounding fictious standards into their heads they can never meet, but the truth is even worse.

Even we weren't enough, and we were celestial beings. We were a thousand times more beautiful. We were stronger and braver than their tiny minds could fathom. Yet here we are, rotting in literal hell surrounded by the smells of melting flesh and excrement and the screams of the tortured gnawing on one another's bones—while they complain, "Oh, that is the worst" of their infantile *hell* of travel delays or trying to navigate an automated phone system to speak to an actual person. Although I must admit, I do enjoy watching Scumtick torment souls using poor customer service as a lesser torture device in the first circle of hell.

Your victim will never be good enough for her kids, let alone for God. Splash some cold reality on that girl's face. Or don't. Reality will bite her soon enough. She will always be judged—especially by her daughter, husband, and friends—anyone close enough to see her flaws. She can give them the best years of her life, sacrifice her body and career, spend countless hours and dollars, wipe their filth and mop up their sick, but they will still complain to their friends and therapist about the one time she didn't listen to their story or the soccer goal she missed because she was chatting with a friend on the sideline. Sure, we demons are expert deceivers, but we don't need to be in this case. When we tell her she isn't good enough, we are the ones speaking the truth!

We made one mistake. That was all it took. Our Enemy didn't care that we spent thousands of years praising Him. All we wanted was a little acknowledgment, a little time in the sun, a little glory for ourselves and we were cast out of paradise forever! Why does she think she would be judged any differently than the rest of creation? I can't believe humans fall for the notion that their whiny, snot-nosed offspring will see and appreciate their sacrifices or, even more ridiculous, that their pathetic efforts will somehow outweigh their innumerable failures. Who's the one peddling lies now?

I know what Our Enemy claims. I know the nonsense those slimy, disgusting earthlings within His protection spout about their sins being washed away, about them being His children. I don't buy it. I know He snatches as many as He can from us, but I can't believe that He really loves them like His own children. He can't. No one could.

They are revolting. They may have been made in His image, but they have distorted it. Like a freak born with two heads or three legs, their resemblance to Him makes them even more repulsive, for at the same moment you can imagine what they should be as well as the horror of what they actually are. I'm sure He has plans for them that we don't know about. Not that it matters to us.

All I know is that I hate Him, and He wants them. The human vermin are His one vulnerability. The one way we can hurt the Divine Enemy who has inflicted so much pain on us is to snatch them from His grasp. Every single soul we drag down into hell with us pains Him.

Once again you show your absolute ineptitude by focusing on the wrong things. That slobbering sentimental claptrap she might use to try to console herself will never be a threat to us. Her temporary comfort will melt away soon enough when reality smacks her in the face.

As it soon will.

If you don't blow it —

Twisttale

ABBY'S JOURNAL

Sunday, January 24th— (part two)

Hold the phone—Jessica's pregnant.

I can't believe I'm writing those words. I can't imagine starting over again at our age. The twins are almost to adulthood. Staring down eighteen more years, starting with wiping poopy bottoms and uncontrollable tantrums (at least twenty-five percent my own) seems unthinkable.

She sprung the news on me today when I tentatively tried to warn her about Lucas while we looked over the spec sheets of all the houses we had just visited. At first, I thought she was kidding. Then I saw the tears well up behind her smile, "Nope. Not kidding."

I blurted out a knee-jerk "Congratulations!" while mentally debating whether "I'm so sorry!" would have been more appropriate. The bustling coffee shop offered minimal privacy for honest conversation.

"How do you feel?" I whispered.

"Like my life is in a tailspin—completely out of control."

"I'm so sorry, friend. What can I do?"

"Tell me what to do." She stared me straight in the eyes. Jessica, who'd raised sarcasm to an art form, spoke with true desperation.

"What do you want to do?"

"I want to go back in time." Her brave smile reappeared, but this time a tear slid down her cheek. "Specifically to Josh's birthday party, but that's not an option, so I've got to figure out a way forward from here."

I knew what I was supposed to tell her as a Christian, didn't I? Abortion is a sin. It's killing another human. It seems so cut and dried when it's theoretical.

But in this case... I didn't know what I was supposed to tell my friend when her world was falling apart. I knew what Josh would say. He would say, "Babies are a precious gift! We'll get through this together. Abby will throw you a baby shower. We'll figure it out." But the words felt callous when I looked into her eyes brimming with tears, when I knew firsthand the pain of childbirth and the years of sacrifice that children demand.

Telling her that nothing matches the sweetness, love, and joy my children bring to my life somehow felt like I would only be pouring salt in the wound.

My mouth went dry. I pressed my lips together and tried to turn up the corners of my mouth as I squeezed her hand. It was all the support I could muster. I heard all the voices in my head. *You have to be supportive of her right to choose. It's her body. She doesn't have to do this. If you're not willing to take her baby, you don't have the right to advise her to keep it.*

For fear of saying the wrong thing, I said nothing.

We finished our chai lattes, and I hugged her as we left. When I got in my car and I was sure she couldn't see me, I surprised myself by bursting into tears, the sobs wracking my body. I felt like a failure—as a friend, as a Christian, as a human.

I still do.

I haven't been able to stop crying. The dam's been breached, and I can't stop the flood. I tell myself to stop thinking about it, yet I can think of nothing else. The voices all sound hollow in the face of the stark reality of my beautiful friend and the new life inside her. I don't know what's right anymore.

Stumbletrick,

Nice, huh? Brilliantly twisted, I like to say—two souls in torment and one more hanging in the balance.

The technique is simple in concept but complicated to execute: turn vices into virtues and virtues into vices.

Vastly superior to slapping down some run-of-the-mill temptation, don't you think? Admit it: convincing a human it's cold-hearted to encourage her friend to let a baby live—it's a pretty magnificent manipulation of their moral compass.

Yet, that's where we are.

So how did we get here, besides my obvious genius, of course? I wouldn't want to *bore* you with dry details you barely understand ... except that's exactly my job! How do you think I got the name Twisttale in the first place? Not because I went the instant gratification route (although I do encourage *that* at every opportunity with our American victims).

No, these things take time and finesse. So, here's the technique. First, determine your victim's passion and gifting. I know, I hate those words. But regrettably, our Enemy didn't create neat little cookie-cutter minions like any rational being would. Instead, He created billions of sloppy, messy little vermin, each motivated a little differently and with their unique strengths and weaknesses. It's infuriating and makes our mission so much harder. However, as stated before, I have made my career on twisting His designs and making them work for us. So, back to the technique. Once you identify their particular forte, start to convince them that it is actually their *weakness*. At the same time, assure them that their greatest weakness is what the world truly needs.

For example, in this case, I've taken one of Abby's strengths—her love of righteousness—and I 've convinced her that it's bad, whispering, "You can't tell others what to do!"

Then, I've taken her weakness—her pride—and I've used it to fuel the worst version of herself. "What am I supposed to say? What's the current, most enlightened view of an unplanned pregnancy?" The brilliance is that I've convinced her that this watered-down version of herself, carefully engineered for the greatest acceptance and societal approval, is her best self. Take some time to think about this one. Admire it for the art that it is.

This is only one example. Don't worry. You'll see lots more.

Learn from the Master Deceiver —

TwistTale

ABBY'S JOURNAL –

Wednesday, January 27th –

I can't.

You name it, I can't.

Get out of bed. Wash my face. Get dressed. Fix dinner. Heck, raising my head feels like a gargantuan feat. It's too much—Jessica, Josh, the kids, Facebook, friends. I can't face any of them.

I asked Ruthie to take care of everything. I only told her I'm not feeling well and I'd pay extra, but I think she suspects the truth. Nothing gets by that woman. If something happens in this house, she knows about it. That usually works in my favor, but now she is undoubtedly judging me. I don't care. I'm judging myself. I'm not going to waste energy trying to determine if her comment about how I must have worn myself out was sincere or meant as a dig. I can't take any more negativity. Heaven knows I already have enough in my head.

This journal entry is the first thing I've managed in three days. Maybe I'll go back to bed now and try to get up tomorrow.

Dear Corel,

Her body's not sick. Her brain's not malfunctioning. It's doing exactly what our Lord designed it to do—signaling to her that something is wrong. She won't die from not eating—at least, not eating for only a few days. Or from crying, either. Human bodies are pretty resilient.

Their hearts are another matter.

She's grieving. She's depressed. She's brokenhearted for her friend—and for herself. The roots of this depression go deep. Jessica was just the trigger. The battle between what she knows to be true and the lies of the enemy is pulling her apart. Her heart whispers that life is sacred and holy, that every soul should be celebrated and revered, and that the weak should be protected by the strong. Yet those thoughts conflict with the screams of a culture that insist that for an adult to have civil rights, those of an unborn baby must be excluded.

Those pills by her bedside table that have kept this monster at bay aren't working anymore. Long-buried hurts are making their way to the surface. But that's okay. Sometimes medicine fixes a problem, and sometimes it only cuts the wires to the warning lights.

Now, at last, she can't deny that there's a problem. Fixing it will take longer, however. We must trust in the slow work of Our Lord. Our hope and trust in Him will never be disappointed. Our Lord will guide us. He never fails.

For His Glory,

Ariam

CHAPTER TEN
Ruthie

ABBY'S JOURNAL

Thursday, January 28th —

This is the absolute last thing I need right now.

As I saw the letter, it felt like one of those moments in the movies when everything else blurs, and the camera focuses in and swivels around a single figure. I read and re-read the first line. "Ruth Darnell vs. Abigail Chrisman..."

Ruthie is suing us.

You have got to be kidding me. She filed a lawsuit? After decades of working in our house and caring for us and our kids, *she* is suing *us*?

I don't even know where to start. We have to hire a lawyer. How much money will that cost? I know my attorney friends charge hundreds of dollars for a single hour. How much paperwork, how much headache? I can't imagine.

Why would she do this? Who put her up to it? Is this because of what I said to her last week in the kitchen? She doesn't really think she'll win, does she? She can't win, can she? *Toxic work environment. Back pay. Emotional pain and suffering. Negligence.* She might as well have thrown in the kitchen sink.

I've been so tormented about what I should or shouldn't do to help Jessica that I haven't been able to think about anything else for days. Now, I'm so angry I might just break this pen. That bitch. That ungrateful, back-stabbing, conniving bitch. Sometimes it's better not to put our feelings down into words. I think I'll put mine into kick-boxing the punching bag in the garage....

Stumbletrick:

Keep it coming from all sides, remember?

This is how it's done when the grown-ups are in charge.

And just wait. We're not done yet.

No Mercy —

Twisttale

Dearest Corel,

Tread carefully. Ruthie is not Abby's enemy, even though she has inflicted a wound.

I don't know all the answers, but I know Ruthie has a good heart. Ruthie and Abby see things differently, which I hope might someday be a source of mutual enrichment. Unfortunately, today is not that day.

We are soldiers, not generals. We don't get to see the entire plan, but we know Our Lord will work even the most painful circumstances together for His good somehow. At the same time, from our Heavenly vantage point, we do see more than Abby does through the knothole of her pain, so we can continue to guide her toward truth.

One thing I'm sure of—our Lord chose you for this assignment. He would not have pulled our most celebrated warrior from the celestial battlefield if He didn't believe your strengths could be decisive in this realm. I have great faith in your abilities.

We can't just snatch her off the crumbling ledge and set her on solid ground at this point. She's heading in the wrong direction for sure, but if you make her troubles disappear, she'll keep going the same way by other means. We are not helping her if we keep her from falling as she travels toward her own destruction. A broken leg or even a broken neck can be a mercy when she's heading toward a worse fate.

Her priorities are upside down. As St. Paul observed, "Their destiny is destruction, their god is their stomach, and their glory is in their shame. Their mind is set on earthly things." Abby often sees the convict, the addict, or even the socially inept as objects of pity or worse. While, in truth, for many of them their sufferings have wiped away their illusions. Often, the ones she disdains have outpaced her on their journey toward Heaven. Perhaps one day Abby might pray, "Bless you, lawsuit," as Alexander

Solzhenitsyn said of the Gulag, "Bless you prison, bless you for being in my life. For there, lying upon the rotting prison straw, I came to realize that the object of life is not prosperity as we are made to believe, but the maturity of the human soul."

Like a butterfly emerging from a chrysalis, Abby needs her struggle. A well-meaning child trying to ease the butterfly's escape could render the insect forever crippled by eliminating the effort required to get the blood pumping into its wings. So be very careful, my dear brother. I know you don't want to prevent her from flying.

For the Glory of our Lord,

Ariam

CHAPTER ELEVEN
Josh

ABBY'S JOURNAL

Friday, January 29th —

I didn't think it could get any worse. What could be worse than being sued by someone you trusted? What could be worse than being stabbed in the back by someone you allowed into your home and into your life? Or facing the possible loss of your home, untold thousands of dollars in legal bills, public embarrassment, mountains of paperwork, and the scrutiny and judgment of the intimate details of your life by strangers?

The betrayal of your husband, that's what.

Et tu, Josh? I thought my life had already reached the bottom. I thought our marriage had already reached the bottom. But then he piled on.

He sided with the housekeeper over his wife! I am absolutely stunned. He can't even be on my side when someone sues us? He can't even have my back when the future of our kids is at stake?

The moment he walked in the door, I called to him, "Josh, you won't believe this—Ruthie is suing us!"

He joined me in the kitchen. "For what?"

"Something about an oppressive work environment, emotional pain and suffering, tripping on a step due to our negligence." I slid the manilla envelope across the island toward him. "It's all written in that legal mumbo-jumbo that makes it impossible to understand. Can you believe she would do that?"

"She must be pretty upset to take such drastic action." He looked at the documents. "I wish she'd have come and talked to us about it first." From his measured tone of voice, you would have thought she'd asked for an extra week of vacation instead of launching an attempt to ruin our lives forever.

"Ya think! If anything, she owes *us*. Think of all the times I have sent her home with leftovers, let her housesit while we were on vacation, or sent home bags of clothes or toys that the twins had outgrown so she could give them to her nieces and nephews. I've given her rides, given her extra work when she needed more cash, and even paid her utilities a few times. And I gave her that nine-month sabbatical you insisted on years ago back when the kids first went to preschool full-time. *I'm* the one with the toxic work environment. I ignore all her smart-aleck comments and never say anything hateful back!"

"And to think that she doesn't appreciate all that," Josh deadpanned. Then he had the nerve to crack a grin.

"Are you not taking this seriously? Or are you trying to justify her poor choices? She's suing us! As in trying to take our money by force and at the very least costing us a lot of money to try to keep it."

He ignored my questions. "There are two sides to every story, Abby. I wonder what happened in her heart that we might not be aware of."

"I can't believe this!" I shouted. "I can't believe you would take *her* side against your own family!"

"I'm not taking sides, Abby." He covered my hand with his. "I *am* trying to see things from her perspective, and I'm hopeful that we can reconcile. Maybe even something good could come out of this for everyone in the end."

"Unbelievable!" I yanked my hand away and backed to the opposite side of the room. I didn't want to be anywhere near him. "That's what I mean. You're *not* taking *our* side! You're not defending your *own wife* and kids. If a thief broke in here with a gun and demanded we leave and give him our house, you would probably say, 'Well, let's look at it from his side. Maybe he needs it more than we do.'"

He walked toward me, his voice getting softer in the same proportion as mine got louder. "Abby, Ruthie's not trying to take our house."

"The hell she isn't!" I almost screamed, stepping away from his outstretched arms. Josh sighed and let his arms fall to his sides—like I'm the one who's a disappointment instead of the man who would leave his family hanging in the wind.

His passivity was infuriating. It meant I have to do all the worrying for both of us. "Actually, it's worse than that. She's more like a ransack-er. She's making sure that if she doesn't have nice things, we can't have them either. Legal fees bankrupt people all the time. She's probably found someone to represent her on a contingency fee, so it's no skin off her nose. She wins either way."

Still Josh said nothing.

I know he has a pure heart, and I love him for that. But when someone is attacking us, I want a champion fighting for me, for our family. I want a hero on a white horse, not a meek and mild peacenik on a donkey singing Kumbaya.

I'm starting to think everyone was right about him.

Stumbletrick,

That's how you drive a wedge. Ready to acknowledge my genius now?

Finally, we're getting somewhere. Can you feel all that delectable hatred and resentment growing in your victim's heart? Without me, you'd still be fumbling around trying to start things back up with her old boyfriend, tempting her to skim funds from the PTA, or pawning her off on some other lame enticement that was never going to pierce her soul. You don't know her at all.

My mouth is watering just thinking about all the damage we can do now. Watch and learn from the master, boy. You have no idea how deep these wounds go. Let me break it down for you. Save this letter for future reference on how to replicate a masterstroke like this.

It's all about expectations.

Ah yes, expectations—the source of so much bitterness and disappointment. Inflate them whenever possible. With Americans, it's so easy! Work that national optimism to your advantage. No matter how much they have, you can convince them they need more—in relationships, possessions, sex, status, romance, fulfillment, sometimes even contentment.

The closer the relationship, the more fodder for hurt. Wives and husbands, parents and siblings, even spiritual brothers and sisters—injuring those tender bonds produces exquisite pain precisely because that's where our victims expect the most love and support. Depending on the circumstances, you can inflict anything from minor irritation to truly crippling angst and gaping wounds.

In this case, we exacerbated things by encouraging her to set her heart on a new house and then twisting her husband's words to play on her deepest fears. But humans don't need our help for ruptures to occur in their relationships. They fail and disappoint one another naturally. Here's the key: we must prevent the repair.

You see, our despicable Divine Adversary has designed the disgusting creatures to grow stronger with difficulties. When ruptures occur, neurons fire red and neural pathways are broken. This causes immediate pain, which can with our help lay the groundwork for years of heartbreak that the pathetic things don't even understand. But all it takes is for one party to admit guilt and humbly ask forgiveness, and the breach could not only be healed, but the bond could be stronger for it. It's so unfair, I know. The Enemy can take all our hard work, twist it, and allow the vermin to *benefit* from it.

Of course, in this case, I've already done the heavy lifting for you again. We started this whole process when she was a child. We inflict the best, most lasting wounds when they are young. That's when we establish the "norm" in their minds around fear and mistrust, lying and deception. Your victim is experiencing that now. She doesn't even know that abandonment, abuse, and neglect in her own early years are causing her husband's words to set her off or why Ruthie's lawsuit elicits such rage.

Ruthie's demon, Muddleweb, has been fanning her resentment and anger as well, but you can't trust other demons so *you* should solidify the victim mentality in Ruthie, too. Reassure her that she isn't acting out of selfishness or vindictiveness but rather following her convictions as a social justice warrior or something along those lines. Oh, the damage we can do when we stoke those self-righteous fires. Speaking of fire, know that we'll be roasting your worthless skin if you mess this up again.

The one who got us back on track —
Twisttale

Dear Corel,

Remember Our Lord chastens the ones He loves when they go astray.

I had hoped we wouldn't need to go here, of course. No parent likes to discipline a child. Parents long to give grace, forgiveness, and mercy. But their children can't receive those things until they repent of their sins. Our Heavenly Father loves Abby too much to let her stay comfortable in her rebellion.

I'm glad that you're asking about Ruthie. You have Our Lord's heart—loving Abby and loving Ruthie, too. Our Lord is not willing that *any* should perish but that all should come to eternal life. It's understandable that Ruthie would seek justice. But for her own sake, she must embrace forgiveness as well.

It's difficult, I know. Wounds this deep are ugly and insidious. But you are right not to judge either of them. That's not our job. That's His realm, and He guards it jealously.

They are both reacting from places of hurt and trauma. Would you judge a fallen comrade who cried out in pain? Our enemy has landed a well-aimed blow at a most vulnerable spot. He's been whispering to Abby for years that no one really loves her, that those in her life only love what she *does* for them. It's why she works so hard to prove her worth, why Josh's perceived criticism cuts so deep. In her eyes, she's an underdog. An outsider. Persecuted even. Despite all her bravado, she's insecure, fearing that she doesn't belong. Now she's convinced she has concrete proof that she's unloved—her greatest fears realized—and no one will be there to protect her when she's threatened. She's convinced she's all alone. We must cut through those lies with the sword of truth.

Human emotions are often not rational. They fear things like spiders, terrorists, shark attacks, and speaking in public while the things they take for granted, like social media, cars, and alcohol, pose the more significant threats.

Ruthie's lawsuit, like a harmless spider, is scary. But no one ever lost their soul from losing money. Quite the opposite, in fact. That doesn't mean Abby isn't in danger, just that she's frightened of the wrong things. She should have been frightened when she lost her way a long time ago.

With guidance from Our Lord we will get her back,

Ariam

ABBY'S JOURNAL

Sunday, January 31st —

"Try to get some rest," Josh said as he pulled a blanket up over my shoulders.

"But I can't." I protested even as I snuggled under the temptingly soft throw. "I need to make dinner and work on a to-do list a mile long. Plus, Sunday is the best day for open houses."

"You stay there. I'll go pick up sushi."

I know he's trying to be helpful, but I've got reports to file, clients to call, checks to mail, bills to pay, emails to write. Oh, and I'd almost forgotten all about working on the happiness commandments with everything else going on. And I haven't even checked in on Jessica.

If I don't keep up the pace, everything will grind to a halt. Who will find us a lawyer? Who will make sure that we don't get taken to the poor house by Ruthie? Somebody's got to keep an eye on things, and I don't see Josh doing it. His calmness is maddening. He acts as if he has some special knowledge that the rest of us lack. I swear, if he starts quoting, "All things work together for good," I'm going to deck him. I don't see God finding us an attorney. Or helping the kids navigate their stuff. Or the thousands of other things I need to do.

And yet, my head is so heavy. I am so tired. Maybe I can trust Josh to take care of things for just a few hours until I get back on my feet again.

Dear Corel,

I love how St Augustine puts it. "They were made for God, and their hearts are restless until they find rest in Him." One little nap and a single moment of trust won't cure all of Abby's ills, but it's an important step in the right direction.

Our enemies want her busy, busy, busy. No time for reflection, meditation, or prayer. No time to consider why she's doing what she does or whether there is a better way toward the peace and contentment she craves. Fill up her days with meaningless drivel until they are gone—that's what the demons seek.

We strive for the opposite. Slow her down. Help her to see the true, the good, and the beautiful all around her. How? Well, one earthly author says they start to reflect when they experience the tastelessness of a passionless life too many times. Perhaps she's finally tired of all her striving after nothing, and she's ready now for a new taste of Heaven. It doesn't take much. Our Lord delights in moving mountains when He sees the smallest mustard seed of faith.

With Joyful Hope in His Glory,

Ariam

Stumbletrick,

Get on task. Take control of your charge. It's all fun and games to get your victim riled up over losing a lawsuit, but this has never been about the relationship between employer and employee. It's about tearing apart a husband and wife as a means to destroy a soul. Forget that at your eternal peril, you fool.

The lawsuit is only valuable to us as a wedge between them. We don't care about whether or not two random vile human vermin get along. Our Enemy Above is the only one who gives a flying flip about such trivialities. We know this marital relationship is strategic. Destroy it, and the dominoes start to fall.

I and your other superiors are not known for our patience. You know what happens when we reach the end of it.

Time is running out—

Twisttale

ABBY'S JOURNAL

Monday, February 1st —

Well, the world didn't fall apart. And those extra few hours of sleep yesterday sure did feel good.

But nothing got done. My to-do list is still there, and I still don't have time enough in the day to do it all. Ruthie is still hot on our heels to destroy our lives. And Josh is still doing nothing to stop her. Everything is still up to me.

So, off to the salt mines. Off to do all I can to provide for and protect my children, to preserve what we've got. If Josh won't lead the charge, maybe he'll at least to let me do it. I'd like to get a little gratitude, a word of thanks, or some appreciation, of course, but I know better than to hope for that from my family. You can't expect it of children until they're grown and have their own kids. And from Josh, I'm just trying to avoid criticism. I've stopped looking for praise.

In the meantime, everybody needs a little encouragement. Since I'm not naïve enough to think I'm gonna get any "attaboys" from anyone else, I'm not going to feel guilty for giving myself a little reward at the end of a long day. Hey, sometimes self-care looks like a bubble bath, sometimes late-night online shopping, and sometimes a pill or a glass of wine or two to help me relax. No judgement.

CHAPTER TWELVE

Storm Brewing

Stumbletrick,

I assure you gluttony is a sin as dangerous as any other, perhaps even more so. If all sins attempt to fill voids, as one irritating but perceptive little French philosopher put it, then it should be evident to you that gluttony is at the heart of a myriad of evils. There's a reason it made the top seven list.

So, by all means, fan every manifestation of this vice—from finishing off the package of cookies by herself in the pantry to binge watching television until the wee hours of the morning to stuffing her closet or padding her bank account. Gluttony is, after all, the original sin—desiring to possess, craving to taste, coveting the forbidden.

Keep telling her it's no big deal. Keep normalizing what should be causing her to hang her head in shame. Send dopamine surging through her brain not only with every bite and sip but with each like on her posts about her wine or chocolate addiction. Let her joke and laugh it off and send funny memes to her friends about tacos and donuts.

Self-control has never been her strong suit. More, more, more is better. Gluttonous eating serves as a simple but satisfying means to destroy that "temple" our Enemy gave them while on earth. But the consequences of this sin are not limited to her waistline. Never let her consider the people in poor countries who made all those clothes that she got for such a deal or where her trinkets and t-shirts will go when they fall apart or she tires of them after three wears.

Best that she never thinks about how those "harmless" habits enslave her. If those thoughts do raise their ugly head, smash them down with the full weight of evil so that she can't bear to venture down that road. Offer her only two choices: either her indulgent behavior must be perfectly acceptable, laudable even, or she must be responsible for infinite human suffering because she bought a $10 top at Target. Given only those two extremes, she'll definitely opt for the former over the rabbit hole of examining the morality of her consumption habits.

She'll continue as she has all these years under my guidance—blindly and robotically consuming, consuming, consuming, attempting to fill the void, but only succeeding in enslaving herself and others even more, never realizing she is constructing her own prison cell until the deadbolt slides in behind her.

We're so close I can almost taste her soul —

Twisttale

ABBY'S JOURNAL

Wednesday, February 3rd —

They say nothing gets your mind off your troubles like helping someone else, so I called Jessica and offered to take her out for a spa day this weekend. Lord knows I could use one, too. I look in the mirror and hate what I see—wrinkles, freckles, bulges and bumps, limp hair, and dark circles under my eyes. I'm sure Josh probably regrets being chained to me. Especially at 7:00 am. Thank goodness for Botox, spandex, and photo filters.

Friday, February 5th —

I don't feel any better. You're supposed to feel better after a good night's sleep, right? You're supposed to know what to do. It's been almost two weeks now, and I am still torn up about Jessica. I want to talk to Josh because he is wise and intuitive about this stuff, but I already know what he'll say, and I feel like that'll put more pressure on me to do things his way.

I figured it wouldn't hurt to confide in a friend for an outside opinion. So, I called Eden.

"What? How? Oh my gosh! That guy she brought to the birthday party, your old boyfriend?"

"Yep," I said. "That's the one. I guess they went out together afterward, and he ended up staying over."

"What's she going to do? She can't afford to have a baby on her own, and why would she even want to?"

"Really, Eden?" My friend's not the deepest person, but her callousness surprised me. "I hope you don't say that to her. My children are the greatest joy of my life."

"But you can afford them," she snapped. "And you can afford for other people to take care of them."

"*I* raised my children, Eden," I responded, barely keeping my temper reigned in as I deliberately pronounced each word.

Eden doubled down. "Raised them maybe, but Ruthie took care of them."

I tried to convince myself that I hung up the phone before saying something I would regret, but honestly, I hung up because I didn't have anything to say.

Ruthie *did* help me raise the kids. She *did* take care of them. I couldn't have done it without her. And I wouldn't have wanted to.

Stumbletrick,

Oh no, you did not.

I was still trying to let you handle at least some small things on your own for a while—sink or swim, show yourself to be of some value, or more likely reveal yourself as completely incompetent. But even with my low expectations, I somehow managed to overestimated you. I never imagined your mismanagement might jeopardize such a well-established operation.

Yet, there you sit, unfathomably oblivious to what you have done. I don't care that she is still binge eating and bought even more kitchen gizmos online she'll never use. You have an almost limitless talent for focusing on precisely the wrong things.

I hate that I have to spell this out for you. Speaking this word makes me nauseated, but I don't see any way around it at this point. So listen up, you imbecile, because I'm not going to repeat myself. You let in *truth*.

Augh! I hate writing that word. I despise it. You should hate it, too. You should jump on it like a flame on dry grass because that's what it is. Instead, you're waxing eloquent about your expected harvest while that single flame is now racing like a wild fire toward the barn.

It's Demoncraft 101. We've been telling her this whole time that Ruthie is her enemy and will destroy her and her family, and more importantly, that Josh is her enemy, too, because he hasn't jumped on the hate-Ruthie bandwagon. Now, one sliver of truth—that she and Ruthie are on the same side, that Ruthie has been her friend—slipped through the breastworks and put all that work in jeopardy. What exactly did you think you were supposed to be doing anyway, if not standing at the ready with buckets of prejudice, racism, and preconceived notions to squelch these flaming arrows?

I mean, we've given you so many options to color Abby's perception of Ruthie. Any one of these would have sufficed:

- she should be grateful to have a job

- no one forced her to take it

- some people are just genetically disposed to nurture or serve, and others to manage

- it doesn't help people to give them handouts, better to make them work for it

- we treat her like family, after all

This last one is one of my favorites because it's dead-on. She expects her family to help when she needs it and doesn't want to pay them extra, either. I could go on and on with the things you could have whispered in her ear. Instead, your failure to recognize the spark has put us all in danger.

Stamp it out, now!

Beyond infuriated —

TwistHale

ABBY'S JOURNAL

Saturday, February 6ᵗʰ —

I called Jessica after we got home from the spa and offered to drive her to Planned Parenthood. Only if she decides to go, of course. I don't want her to go. No one truly wants more abortions. But it's her choice, and my Christian duty is to love her regardless, right?

She asked me if I would loan her the money to help pay for the procedure.

I didn't know what to say. It's one thing to support her decision and offer to drive her, but to give her the money? That might be a bridge too far. I don't think Josh would ever forgive me if he found out. And it would be harder to hide than just driving her and holding her hand.

"I'm sorry, Jessica. I don't think I can."

Silence.

"It's too much," I continued. "Josh would find out. Things are already so tenuous between us. I haven't even told you the latest about Ruthie, but it's pretty bad. He'd be super upset with me even driving you there if he knew."

"You haven't told him?" she asked.

"You know how he is. He always thinks everything is going to be okay. He isn't realistic. He would tell you how children are such a blessing and a joy, that you could do it, that we would help you, or that so many families would love to give a new baby a home. He would start calling it Junior."

I hoped that last sentence would make her laugh, but I only heard silence again on the other end of the phone. I hope I hadn't offended her.

"He doesn't understand," I added after a long pause.

"Maybe I should talk to Josh." Her voice broke with something between a laugh and a cry.

Wow. I wasn't expecting that. "If you want to," I stammered. I wasn't sure if she wanted me to take her seriously or not. "But I think it will only make you feel worse."

"It's hard to imagine I could feel any worse, Abby."

"Okay then. Why don't you come over tomorrow night?"

Good grief. Now I have to tell Josh about the whole thing. As if our lives weren't complicated enough.

Sunday, February 7th —

"Thank you for telling me." Josh sat across from me, elbows on the table and leaning forward as I spelled out the situation.

"It was Jessica's idea. I didn't want to involve you." The harshness of the words, when uttered aloud, surprised me. I would hate it if he shut me out like that.

But even the cold words were less cruel than my true thoughts: *I don't need your approval in order to help my friend. I can make my own decisions about what's right and wrong.*

He stood up. "Of course, Abby. I would love to talk with Jessica. I'm sure she could use some reassurance and encouragement."

"Okay," My words followed him as he walked away. "But when she comes over tonight, I'm not going to be part of the conversation. That's between you and her. I don't want her to think I'm pressuring her one way or the other. I'll support her no matter what she decides."

He stopped, turned around, and gave me a look like I just kicked a puppy. I wasn't sure if he was sad, disappointed, or angry. Regardless, I don't need that judgment. I'm trying to be a good friend. As if he read my mind, he asked, "If you were Jessica, wouldn't you want a friend by your side?"

"I wouldn't want my friend imposing her version of morality on me when I'm the one who has to live with the consequences," I shot back.

"No matter what happens, we all have to live with the consequences."

At the time, I thought he sounded like some irritating holier-than-thou, mountain-top guru.

But his words kept echoing in my mind, swirling around with random quotes from poets, philosophers, and activists I'd heard over the years. Like John Donne's "do not ask for whom the bell tolls," the haunting lyrics of U2's *One*, "We get to carry each other," or heartbroken Mamie Till's plea after her son's brutal murder, "What happens to any of us, anywhere in the world, had better be the business of us all." Finally, I couldn't help but admit the truth. We are all connected. What one does affects all the rest.

Dang it, I hate it when he's right.

Stumbletrick,

We've got a lot in play—her friend's pregnancy, her employee's lawsuit, her husband's disapproval. Throw in all the other fun torments like the new house obsession, social media addiction, compulsive eating, and social anxiety, and we've got quite the storm brewing. All the more reason for you to pay close attention to my instruction.

A novice might be overconfident. At least you're not susceptible to that flaw. Small comfort, as you seem to be leaning in the other direction. Try to keep your cool and follow my guidance. The tree is swaying. No time to lose focus.

Timber —

Twisttale

ABBY'S JOURNAL

Tuesday, February 9th —

The lawsuit is bad enough. Lord knows writing that retainer check for the attorney made me sick, and who knows how much we'll shell out before this is all over. But that's not the worst of it. If I fight this, I'm going to lose Josh. How can we possibly stay together when we're pulling in opposite directions? I don't know what he thinks we *should* do, but it's not fighting this ridiculous lawsuit tooth-and-nail, which means he's not on *my* side. Of all the things that might drive us apart, I never thought it would be him choosing the feelings of our middle-aged housekeeper over the kids and me.

He doesn't see it that way, of course.

"Abby, don't you trust me?" Josh asked as I turned away from him and continued stirring the pasta on the stove. "Don't you think that I will provide for you and the kids? Have I ever not?"

"Of course, you have," I answered. *Which is why Ruthie's suing us.* "It's not about trusting you. It's about fairness. And betrayal. It's about *her.*"

"Okay then, what's our priority? What are the two greatest commandments? To love God and love our neighbors. Let's do that. Let's love Ruthie. Let's try to see it from her perspective and find a way to help her."

Yes, he really said that. What am I supposed to do with someone so unrealistic? The man lives with his head in the clouds. This is reality—real money, a real lawsuit—and Ruthie has made herself our *real* enemy.

It is bad enough that she is trying to take our money. Now, she may cost me my marriage.

Wednesday, February 10th —

Oh, my goodness, I had the most terrible thought. What if Ruthie's intention in the first place was to destroy our marriage? What if she filed the lawsuit because she *knew* it would drive a wedge between Josh and me? In all these years, the thought that Ruthie would have a romantic interest in Josh or vice versa had never popped into my mind. I don't know why— except that they have absolutely nothing in common.

But maybe that's not true. I've never thought of Josh as a minority, but he's not white and neither is Ruthie. His family's Middle Eastern. I've never had much interest in that part of the world, except maybe to travel to Israel someday. We met in England, so I think of Josh as English, if anything.

No, I can't go there. That's crazy. Josh may not like me all the time, and we might disagree on how to respond to this lawsuit, but he would never cheat on me. And she couldn't possibly think he would be interested in her.

Dear Stumbletrick,

Don't.

Don't. Even. Think about touching this third rail. You have proven you lack finesse and good instincts, let alone the intellect to grasp something as complicated as race relations in America.

Satisfy yourself with reaping the fruits of the labor of greater demons like me. If humans can binge watch their favorite shows with no clue how flat screens work, or rev their engines with only the vaguest idea about internal combustion, you can enjoy deeply-rooted racism without understanding the centuries of groundwork, countless layers of deception, warping of theology and politics, or depths of psychological intricacies involved.

Just stay the hell away. Don't even think about touching the wires in the back of this machine, let alone cracking it open.

You are on a strict need-to-know basis. And this is what you need to know, broken down for a simpleton like yourself: encourage haughtiness. Think you can handle that? As long as she continues to think she's better than Ruthie, we're in good shape. The same goes for Ruthie, by the way.

Think of it as the fuel that keeps a high-performance engine running. Keep filling up the tank. You didn't design it, and you don't need to understand it, but even the most amazing engine in the world won't work if it runs out of gas. This is your only job. The fuel that powers this engine of racism is pride, which Americans have in spades.

Don't mess it up.

You exhaust me —

Twisttale

Dearest Corel,

I know it's difficult to understand why some humans on earth seem to think they are superior because of their skin color. In Heaven, the rainbow of colors and hues of God's children shine more beautifully than the flowers of any garden. An exquisite scarlet rose would never claim superiority over a lavishly cascading wisteria. They are masterpieces within themselves and even more beautiful when together.

Unfortunately, the tendrils of this deeply-rooted deception wrap around Abby's entire identity. These interwoven lies, strengthened by centuries of growth, now encircle and invade her mind, heart, and even her relationship with Josh. We can't go in and slice through a web of deception like this in one fell swoop without inflicting even more damage. It's too entrenched.

We know the sword of truth can cut through any lie, no matter how artfully crafted or tightly wound round the heart of the deceived. But we must sever the cords with care and separate the truth from the lies. Is Abby loved by God? Was she chosen for a specific destiny? Has she been blessed? Yes! Absolutely. Is she exceptional? Yes, because she is a child of Our Heavenly Father. Because she was made in His image. Because she is loved by Him and worthy of His ultimate sacrifice.

Here's the tragedy and the lie: Abby thinks those things are a little more true of her than Ruthie. She thinks she's better. She thinks she's prettier, wealthier, more loved, more desirable, more deserving, smarter, harder working, more virtuous—better. Throughout her life, Abby's beliefs have been reinforced by her own actions and by the culture around her over and over again. And Ruthie knows it.

Abby's pride has permeated their every interaction, consciously and subconsciously, from the moment Ruthie walked up the sidewalk to

Abby's house for the job interview to their latest clash over the lawsuit, plus every conversation and decision in between. Abby's superiority complex complicates even the occasional kindness or generosity she shows Ruthie, leaving Abby feeling as if she gets extra credit for being nice even though her sacrifice is minimal. Although Abby would never utter the words, her actions proclaim her belief that "God loves us all, but He likes me better."

No, we won't conquer this enemy in a single battle. However, that doesn't mean we won't fight it, only that we have to cut her loose one strand at a time.

Always in your corner,

Ariam

CHAPTER THIRTEEN

Shirley

ABBY'S JOURNAL

Sunday, February 14th —

The girls invited me to Sunday brunch this morning. I'm surprised they asked. I make a point of telling them we go to church every week. Growing up, we went three times each week, so I always felt guilty if I didn't drag the kids there at least on Sunday mornings.

But Josh surprised me. "You should go if you want."

I don't know what to make of that man sometimes. He's the one who didn't like skipping church for the kids' soccer games, but now he encourages me to play hooky? Maybe this has something to do with Jessica. Out of respect for her privacy, I hadn't reached out to her since their conversation last week. I figured I'd let her come to me.

"I can't do that," I protested. "How would it look? To the girls? To the folks at church?"

"I think it would look like you care about your friends." Josh handed me a cup of coffee. "Jessica could really use some encouragement."

You see what I'm up against? I can't win. If I turn down the invitation, I'm heartless. If I accept, I look like a godless hypocrite who skips Sunday School for mimosas.

But I do like mimosas, so brunch with the girls it was! Even better with Josh's blessing.

Outside the restaurant, I ran into Shirley. She looked ridiculous, which isn't unusual for her. She had tied an oversized scarf around her head and knotted it under her chin. It trailed down her back and, along with the weight she's gained, made her look like an ancient European beggar woman. I almost didn't recognize her shuffling along the sidewalk with her bags and oxygen tank.

She greeted me with a great big hug, using a volume and invoking the name of God just a notch above the socially-acceptable level, "Abby! What a blessing to see you! Thank you, God!"

"Hi Shirley," I answered in a much quieter tone hoping she would imitate. "How have you been?"

"Better than I deserve. God is taking care of me like always. So many blessings. So, how are you and the twins? How's my goddaughter Destiny?"

"We're good. We were sad to hear you are sick."

"Oh, we're all dying. Some of us just get reminded more often. I'm not going to let it steal my joy."

"Are you getting any visitors?"

I hadn't meant to volunteer—I kind of meant visitors from far away. I never know what to say when people are in crisis.

But Shirley jumped all over it, "I'd love for you to come visit! It's been too long. Drop by anytime. I'm almost always home. It's so hard for me to get out nowadays." I promised I would, mostly to get away and on to brunch with the girls. But now I have to add a visit to Shirley to my list of things to do.

Stumbletrick,

You're such a rube. You want accolades because your victim didn't go to church this morning? Are you kidding? Do you think that we'd let her keep going to church every week unimpeded all these years if we thought it was a threat? I do some of my very best work in American churches.

Don't confuse the church where your victim attends with the meetings of Christians in the Eastern hemisphere. You would definitely be a fool to allow your victim into places like that. Best case scenario, she would leave with new protections against your darts and arrows. Worst case, you'd leave with skin burning, eyes blinded, and a severe case of PTSD. But this is the West.

Most American churches today resemble a country club or a concert—depending on your flavor—more than a place of worship. We can waltz right in without so much as a headache. No one will even suspect you are there. Try that in a real house of prayer, and see how far you get. Of course, anywhere believers gather to pray or worship our Enemy is dangerous, but you would be surprised how few truly do that. Have you not yet heard the old adage that there's more sin in church on Sunday mornings than in the bars on Saturday night? I haven't actually measured to see if that's true, but I'm sure the agnostics in the bars are more aware that they are sinning than the church-goers in the pews falling prey to our old traps of pride, judgement, and deceit.

Even their "worship" songs often focus more on themselves and how they feel than praising God. That's if they are paying attention to the words at all instead of thinking about the people around them, what they will be doing later, or critiquing everything from the production quality of service to the temperature of the air. Like everything, freedom of religion has its pros and cons. I remember debating that issue in demon training. I think you were in that class. Surely, you must be somewhat familiar with our religious protocols. I don't have time to go into all of them in this letter, but they are hardly isolated to America. Demons have been doing excellent work inside churches with religious people for millennia all the way back to the moneychangers in Solomon's temple.

Shirley, however, is a problem.

A serious problem.

You need to nip that in the bud,

TwistTale

Dear Corel,

Wonderful news! I'm so delighted to hear about Shirley—how I love her! What a powerful ally she will be in our fight. Let's do everything you can to make sure they spend time together. That's exactly what our poor Abby needs—better voices speaking truth and grace into her life. A few piercing words of truth from a trusted friend can do much to cut through those lies wrapped around our girl's heart.

As for brunch with girlfriends instead of sitting through a sermon at church, highly irregular, I know. But what did Our Lord say? "The Sabbath was made for man, not man for the Sabbath." We're in rescue mode like when David was fleeing from King Saul. While I applaud your desire to help Abby honor all Our Lord's commands, sometimes we have to prioritize the greatest—love your neighbor and love God—over the others.

It's entirely likely that Abby will be doing more loving and relationship building at brunch with her girlfriends than she would have been if she had gone to church this morning. We have to stay focused on our mission. Once we save her marriage, we can follow up and find her a better church. I'm sure Shirley can help us with that as well. But first things first. We've got to cut through the lies. Relationships, rather than institutions, do that best.

For His Glory,

Ariam

ABBY'S JOURNAL

Monday, February 15th —

Brunch with the girls didn't go quite as I expected.

Running into Shirley made me late, so they had already grabbed a table. Eden waved her mimosa in my direction to get my attention. As I slid into the high-backed booth, Ivy said, "Jessica has caught us all up to speed."

I wasn't sure whether she was referring to Ruthie or the pregnancy, so I let them lead the conversation. "It's so awful," Eden commiserated.

"Yes, it is," I answered, still not sure of the topic of conversation.

"What are you going to do?" asked Jessica, trying to clue me in on what she had told them—and what she had not.

As indignant and angry as I had been about Ruthie's lawsuit and Josh's reaction, and as cathartic as it normally would have been to rehash it with the girls, knowing that Jessica was bearing a secret burden greater than mine took all the wind out of my sails. After my somewhat lackluster recounting of my grievances, Jessica leaned over and laid her head briefly on my shoulder in feigned sympathy for my plight. Recognizing her gesture as coded thanks for keeping silent, I pressed my head against hers and squeezed her hand in genuine sympathy for her own predicament.

I've been thinking about it all weekend. I would never, ever admit this out loud to anyone, but maybe Ruthie has a point. I probably shouldn't have said anything about her unpatriotic comments in front of the kids.

And there have been times over the years when I probably took advantage of her, expecting her to work late or come in early when I needed her, and she wasn't really in a position to say no. I could have treated her with more respect. What do they call those things nowadays, microaggressions? I'm sure I'm probably guilty of a ton of those. I just don't know what they are. But that's the problem, right? I never put any time or effort into figuring it out. I was more focused on myself, didn't really care all that much about what she wanted, and assumed she should have to conform to our way of doing things. I've never taken the time to celebrate or acknowledge (or even think about) her contributions to our family. And then, of course, the twins picked up on my attitude.

Cash has never been particularly deferential to anyone. I love that boy dearly, but like most teenage boys he does his own thing without too much thought for anyone else. He's even worse now that he's in college, getting ideas about being a captain of industry as well as captain of the debate team.

Destiny is another story, however. Ruthie's been with us since just after the twins were born and I'm sure she thinks of Destiny as almost her own daughter. And Destiny probably considers Ruthie at least half as much her mother as me. Of course, for our little prima donna that means Ruthie exists to make her life easier. Ruthie used to joke, "I don't work for Abby. I work for that little girl."

I did lean on her pretty hard when they were little—long hours and letting her do all the really awful stuff like the vomit, poop, and tantrums that I didn't want to deal with myself. But man, those years were hard on all of us—two babies crying, money tight. It's hard to give what you don't have.

We're not perfect. We could have been nicer. But I thought we were all in this together. I think we both miss the children they used to be now that they're off on her own. Without them to care for and demanding so much of our attention, we don't have as much of a united purpose.

I still can't believe she's suing us, though! We gave her a job for years—a steady salary, meaningful work. We even occasionally included her in family celebrations. Heck, for a few years, she lived with us. What did she expect? For us to adopt her? Promise her an inheritance? We did the best we could.

Tuesday, February 16th —

I kept my promise to visit Shirley today.

Shirley is both super easy and super hard to be with. When she's happy, she's great. She oozes positive energy, loves to laugh, and would give you the shirt off her back.

But when she's not, boy, lock the door and turn out the lights. She's not afraid to break right through societal conventions. You never know what she might do or say. Or ask. Because of that, I generally hold her at arm's length until I know which Shirley she's going to be.

Today, thank goodness, she was the easy-to-love Shirley. Before I was even through the door, she was struggling to her feet.

"Hi, honey! I'm so glad you came! How are you?" She was one of the only people who wanted to know the honest answer.

"Don't get up! We're the same as always." Not quite an honest answer, but I didn't plan to get into all the gritty details today. "Busy, busy, busy. How about yourself?"

She ignored that. "We'll come back to you in a minute. How are the twins?"

I resisted the strong temptation to spend the entire time waxing eloquent about Destiny and Cash or our latest drama with Ruthie. "Shirley, I didn't come here to tell you a bunch of boring details about us. I came to see you."

She opened her mouth wide in a big, bold laugh, "Ha!" and reached out to squeeze my hand as I sat next to her. She used a wheelchair a lot now and had been on oxygen for months, but today she had set up camp on the loveseat. The cozy living room overflowed with memorabilia of a life well-lived—floor-to-ceiling bookshelves stuffed full of books as well as photos, posters, hand-written notes, and small tokens that might look odd to strangers but each represented wonderful stories I'd heard from Shirley through the years. Marie Kondo would have hyperventilated, but I found myself breathing easier than I had for a while.

We reminisced about the good times, and I was reminded why I love Shirley. I knew her long before I ever met Josh. She was there for me when I was single—maybe a little too loud at times, a little too *much*, a little too crazy for my milquetoast taste, but when I needed help, she came to my rescue.

I called her when rainwater had been running down my kitchen wall. She showed up wearing a black plastic garbage bag over her clothes, and together in the pouring rain, we climbed on the roof to clean out the overflowing gutters. When no one else was brave enough to tell me when my neckline was too low, my dress too see-through, or my boyfriend a louse, Shirley didn't hesitate. Back when I was still in the career grind, she brought me dinner when I was too swamped to leave the office, so we could spend a few minutes together.

Our friendship involved more than her coming to my rescue, though. We also had fun together. Shirley loves to have fun. We took road trips, she taught me to fish, we made Oreo cookie ice cream milkshakes, and she planted tulips in my front yard. No one has ever been a bigger cheerleader for me.

With all the times she had helped me, you'd think I would have been more grateful. And I was. But to be honest, she sometimes scares me. She can be a little too forward, ask too much, expect too much. In fact, she can be downright impossible. She has no boundaries. She gives her all to those she loves, and she hurts when it isn't returned. I can't always love her like she wants or deserves.

"How's Ruthie?"

The question jolted me. Sitting and laughing with Shirley had driven my troubles with Ruthie far from my mind. The usual "Oh, she's fine" almost rolled off my tongue before something stopped me.

By fashion magazine standards, no one would ever call Shirley a beauty. Built more like a linebacker than a runway model, she took up more than her fair share of the loveseat. When she smiled, she showed a row of tiny teeth, and her plump cheeks almost hid her sparkling eyes. Even with her thinning gray hair, double chin, and oxygen tube, she still grinned more like a mischievous child than a middle-aged woman, whose body was now failing her.

She smiled at me now, waiting for my response, and I thought I'd never seen anything more beautiful in my life. Beautiful Shirley, a true friend, always ready to share in my joys and pain, happy to listen to my stories, shoulder my burdens, and help me in any way she could. Why had I let so much time go since I'd last visited?

So I poured out my heart. I told her all about Ruthie—the anger, the resentment, the fear, the jealousy, the pride—as much as I knew how. "What should I do?" I asked finally as I wiped away the tears flowing down my face.

"Wait."

"Wait for what?" I asked, confused.

"Listen."

"Listen to what?" I pressed, already guessing I wasn't going to like her answer.

"Listen to her, to others, to God. Think about what Ruthie wants. Think about what you've done. Then go to her." After a pause, she lowered her voice and squeezed my hand. "Humble yourself."

Now I remembered why I had let so much time go between visits to Shirley. I really wanted to pretend that I didn't hear her advice. I wanted to gloss right over it, to discount it as the ramblings of a crazy lady. But her words cut through the armor and lodged deep in my heart.

I shifted in my seat. "Okay." I took a deep breath, considering how this might work. "Maybe I could get my thoughts together and then call her."

"No. You need to go to her. Don't send an email or call. Go to her house. Look her in the eye."

"Really?"

"Yes, really."

So now I have to go to Ruthie's house.

Stumbletrick,

It's like you're not even a demon! Are you sure there's not a smooth-skinned human biped hiding behind those cracked teeth or under your gnarly horns and wart-covered face?

We, of all creatures, should know that appearances can be deceiving. How were you snookered by that doddering facade? Allowing any contact between your victim and that predator is cause for disciplinary action, but letting your victim actually go to her house is inexcusable.

Since you have exhibited exactly zero common sense thus far, let me spell out next steps for you. Don't let them *talk* to one another!

Yes, a face-to-face confrontation could devolve into a delicious catfight. But honest, direct communication could also punch a hole in those carefully-crafted narratives we've been nurturing. Don't risk it.

Instead, fan the flames of bitterness and resentment on both sides. Pile on fear and jealousy. Let each imagine that she knows the other's heart. Remind them of the wrongs they have suffered (or perceive to have suffered). Keep bringing up those wounds. Even better, let them inflict more. At this point, they are so suspicious and prone to expect the worst from each other that the slightest look or word could widen the divide. Any demon worth his salt could stoke their suspicions into juicy hate-filled thoughts, with or without any real facts.

Now I'm just doing your job for you. Figure it out and report back.

Do better or else—

Twisttale

Dear Corel,

Oh, my goodness, I'm on the edge of my seat! Excellent work, dear Guardian. So much fantastic news in your latest report. Little by little, we're breaking through the lies! Abby is starting to look at things from the perspective of others—especially Ruthie's. Fantastic! Her conversation with Shirley was exactly the jolt she needed. I love how you helped orchestrate their "chance" meeting!

It's too soon to celebrate, of course, but take heart. Your labors are having the desired effect. Pointing our girl in the right direction doesn't automatically mean she'll get there, but it's so much better than before.

No doubt our enemies will have seen our progress and will be redoubling their efforts to deceive her. I know you will remain vigilant, dear soldier, against their attacks. Press on! Protect and guide our girl down that straight and narrow path. She needs you more than ever.

Our prayers are ever with you,

Ariam

CHAPTER FOURTEEN

Ash Wednesday

ABBY'S JOURNAL

Wednesday, February 17th —

I went to Ruthie's today. The walk to her front door was the longest, hardest journey of my entire life.

As I lifted the steel latch of the chain-linked gate, I clicked the remote on my car for a second time just to make sure I'd locked it. I took a deep breath and tried to keep nervous tears from forming in my eyes. "No one is looking at you," I lied to myself even as I saw the neighbors watching me with curiosity and suspicion. The residential street was full of noise—loud music playing from an open window, children yelling, teenagers standing outside laughing. The bark of a dog suddenly reminded me that I didn't know if Ruthie had one. I paused for a moment before stepping into the yard in case a vicious canine came barreling around the corner.

As I stood waiting for the invisible dog, a loud voice called in my direction. "Hey!"

I started toward the door again.

"Hey you, ...lady!" The young woman sitting on the neighboring porch with some friends would not be ignored. I glanced her way as she rose out of her chair. "You're not allowed to park there!"

My cheeks burned and my eyes watered, embarrassed for my mistake and humiliated by my tears over something so trivial.

This was too hard. I couldn't do it. I didn't belong. This was why I had never gone to Ruthie's house before. Everything in me wanted to turn around, get in my car, drive away, and never come back.

But I had to do this. I had followed Shirley's advice last night: I waited and listened. I hadn't liked what I heard, but it was clear: this was part of my penance for the wrongs I had done to Ruthie. I said in my humblest tone, "I'm sorry. I didn't know. Where am I supposed to park?"

"Not in front of a fire hydrant," the girl yelled back. "Geez! I didn't mean to make you cry!" She barked a derisive laugh as she turned back toward her friends, no longer interested in where I parked.

I took a moment in the car to compose myself before moving it a few dozen feet forward. The length of my walk of shame had now doubled. Maybe that was good. Perhaps it would give me more time to get in the right state of mind before I met Ruthie.

I gritted my teeth and forced my feet to take each step down the cracked, uneven sidewalk toward Ruthie's gate.

This time I made it all the way to the porch. Avoiding the untrustworthy-looking chipped iron railing, I climbed the concrete steps. I raised my hand to knock on the glass of the aluminum screen door, but Ruthie had seen me coming. Probably the whole neighborhood had seen me coming.

"Hello, Abby." Her tone and expression were neutral. "Why don't we sit out here on the porch?"

"Okay." I wasn't sure if I was relieved or offended not to be invited inside her home, and I pushed back my natural inclination to interpret it as a slight.

Now thankful for the noisy neighborhood din surrounding us, I sat on a faded metal chair flecked with rust, placing my purse in my lap for lack of a better spot. Ruthie sat opposite and gazed toward the cars parked along both sides of the street. For once in her life, it looked like she was going to let me take the lead.

"I was hoping we could work this out without lawyers," I began.

"I'm sure you were," she replied.

"Our attorney told me not to talk to you."

"Yet here you are—doing just what you want anyway."

I closed my eyes, pressed my lips together, and turned the palms of my hands up under my purse on my lap. Someone once taught me to do that to try to control anger. *I'm trying so hard here, Ruthie, please meet me halfway.*

"It wasn't easy for me to come here...."

"I've had to do a lot of things that weren't easy. Maybe it's your turn."

I opened my mouth to respond then closed it. This wasn't going the way I had hoped. For the second time in five minutes, I wanted nothing more than to retreat. Get up and walk away. Leave Ruthie and this whole place behind.

I would say we sat in silence for a few moments, but I don't think her neighborhood is ever silent. Finally, I asked, "Do you want me to leave?"

"If you're finished." Then after a pause, she added, "I don't know what you came here to do. I imagine you haven't done it yet. If so, I'd prefer you get on with it."

"I came to say I'm sorry."

"Sorry that I'm suing you? Sorry that people might know how you treated me? Sorry people might criticize you? You never could stand that. What exactly are you sorry for?"

"I'm sorry things turned out this way," I whispered, the tears welling up again. "I'm sorry that it took me so many years to see you for who you are, for us to have this conversation."

I wanted to look Ruthie in the eye like Shirley told me to, but I couldn't quite yet.

"So, who is it that you think I am now?"

"My equal," I confessed, laying bare what last night's meditation revealed to me, fully realizing what the painful admission implied I had not believed before.

She took her time responding, letting the words sit between us. But instead of worry, I felt peace. My burden lifted. My breath came easier, no longer stifled by the weight pressing on my chest. I waited silently for her response.

"I suppose you think I'm going to drop the lawsuit now?"

"I wish you would, but I needed to apologize regardless of what happens on that front. I had hoped we could talk. I don't know how else to start to heal some of the broken places."

"Are you really going to listen if I talk? You're not going to interrupt and make excuses and defend yourself?" Ruthie knew me well.

"I'll try."

"Like you've *been* trying? Isn't that what you always say, 'I tried my best'? I'm afraid this time you're not going to get what you want."

"What do you want me to do, Ruthie?"

The question hung in the air for at least thirty seconds, but it felt like much longer. Months. Years.

"I want you to respect me," Ruthie finally said. "I want you to acknowledge how your actions hurt me. It feels fair to me that you should pay a price for that."

I gulped at her mention of a price, feeling the defensive arguments forming in my head, wanting to argue that I had done the best I could at the time. Wait, no. She was right. My best wasn't enough. I touched the cross around my neck and offered up a one-breath prayer for help. Suddenly, I felt a sense of calm and clarity about our relationship, like the future between us might be OK somehow after all.

"Ruthie, would you come to dinner at our house so we can talk about some of your grievances? You know me—too well, probably. Left to myself, I'm sure I would fall back to my old habits of getting defensive and making excuses, and I don't want to do that. Having Josh there will help us both keep things in perspective."

Ruthie turned and for the first time in our conversation looked directly at me. I forced myself not to look away from her dark brown eyes.

"We can do that."

"Thank you." I was so relieved that I wanted to hug her. I wanted this rift to be healed. But I knew it wasn't, not yet, and that I wasn't going to be able to navigate this minefield alone. Rather than stay and risk screwing everything up, I rose to go. "I'll call you to confirm details. Maybe a week from Friday night?"

"That should be fine."

Walking back toward the car, the sounds of the neighborhood—music, yelling, and laughter—no longer seemed threatening. I smiled at the skinny boy who crossed in front of me chasing a stray ball and waved to the girls on the porch next door. I couldn't wait to get home to my safe, quiet neighborhood, but it felt like a victory had been won. For the first time in years, I felt hope and joy after a conversation with Ruthie and couldn't wait to tell Josh and Shirley.

Dear Corel,

I had high hopes when our prince, Archangel Michael, gave you this assignment. I knew you would be able to break through those webs of deception! Tears of joy stream down my face as I write. I know it's not the end. I know we have far to go, and you know we'll continue to pray, but it is such a blessing to be able to share this sweet victory with you!

Precious Abby has begun to acknowledge her wrong and see the need to change. Her prayer on the porch in her moment of need reverberated throughout Heaven, and what joy I felt when God's grace and love immediately flowed through her soul. Praise to the Lord Almighty for those crucial first steps toward new life! Hallelujah! Amen! May it ever be so.

But we must not let down our guard. Both Ruthie and Abby are incredibly vulnerable. Our enemies will be ramping up their forces to stamp out these tiny seeds of healing and reconciliation to prevent them from experiencing any more of the abundant life Our Lord desires for them. May the Lord strengthen you and continue to bless His wayward children.

For His Glory,

Ariam

Stumbletrick,

I don't have time to berate you properly for this colossal screw-up. I trust even you recognize the severity of the situation. I had her halfway to hell and you let her pray, and no ordinary prayer. It was a direct and sincere call for help from the Enemy.

I wish I could torment you right now myself, but we need all hands on-deck. We've got to pivot. I've got two words for you: false accusation. It's one of the many tools in my bag of tricks that I've perfected over the centuries. It's practically idiot-proof, which is perfect for you. But unfortunately, we all know that even if I spell it out in excruciating detail, odds are you will still find a way to mess it up.

I won't be found derelict in *my* duties, though, so here's the plan. Think about your victim going along, trying hard to do better. Then wham! Sucker-punch her with an allegation for a crime she didn't commit.

Before she recovers her balance from the shock of being condemned and judged for something she didn't even do, start heaping on the shame. "They think you're a [liar, thief, narcissist, racist, or whatever]. You should run and hide. You can never show your face to them again." You have no idea how many people we have removed from the danger of church and human community this way.

If the shame doesn't have her crumpling to her knees trying to crawl away from the pain and breaking her human connections—our ultimate goal, of course—then start laying on condemnation as well. So to recap: in addition to tormenting her with the shame that everyone thinks she's at fault, convince her that she is guilty of the false accusation as well. "You *are* selfish. You *are* a screw-up. It's no surprise that they saw through you. You can't do anything right, no matter how hard you try. You are a fraud,

and as soon as anyone gets close enough to you, they will figure that out."
Got it?

My bet is the self-condemnation will lay her out flat. She is weak and pathetic. You could have her wallow in the torment, playing the tapes over and over in her mind—debilitating and painful, a solid option. But remember, her desperate desire to ease her mental torture is also a perfect opportunity to introduce a new vice or solidify an old addiction.

Consider what she is most susceptible to and combine that with what is most enslaving. For instance, given her history it wouldn't take much of a push to have her drowning her sorrows with a pint, or half-gallon, of ice cream. That's an easy option. As I've said before, too many ineffective demons underestimate how enslaving emotional eating can be. But don't always settle for ice cream. Is her pain so acute and her desire for escape so strong that perhaps a bottle of wine would be better? Or, instead of using food and alcohol as drugs, she could just skip to the real thing. Press in on that pain, then suggest a couple of pills might make it disappear for a while.

Get creative, you moron. I'm already practically doing your job for you. I know alcohol and drugs are old staples, tried and true. It's hard even to quantify the amount of human suffering they've caused. But that doesn't mean there aren't other equally damaging (and addictive) options—sex, porn, and lust, for example. I could see your girl losing herself in a lusty novel (or two or three) then perhaps watching the film version. As an added bonus, that option will sow more seeds of discontentment in her marriage as well.

All this potential progress springs from what seems like such a small thing, a false accusation. I didn't even get to the damage we could do with pride and righteous indignation because I don't think your human vermin will be able to crawl her way past the shame and condemnation. Then again, I have found it difficult to overestimate your incompetence.

Because time is of the essence, your victim needs to be falsely accused by a real person and fast. We could use social media to slowly torture and debilitate her through a constant state of lower-grade shame, sapping her will to live by constantly berating her, but that is more of a slow-cooker meal. We need that human flame broiled, so find someone to light the fire right under her derriere, or I'll light one under yours.

Get cooking—

TwistTale

ABBY'S JOURNAL

Thursday, February 18th —

I broke the news to the family over our monthly Sunday night dinner together.

"I thought we weren't supposed to be speaking to Ruthie," Destiny protested.

"*You* are not going to be speaking to her. Your dad and I are. You guys don't live here anymore, remember?"

"This is wonderful news, Abby!" Josh was beaming across the table. "I'm so glad to hear you and Ruthie have been talking. It will be good to see her and hear how she's feeling."

Why do I find even his accolades slightly grating? I feel like I did a really hard thing, made a really big step forward, and he's still mostly concerned about Ruthie's feelings. I tried to push back the negative thoughts, giving him the benefit of the doubt. He probably doesn't realize how he sounds.

"This is so typical of you, Mom," Destiny said.

"What do you mean?"

"You think a dinner invitation can fix a lawsuit. You think the rules don't apply to you. You try to bend everything to fit what you want. You do it to me all the time."

Josh intervened. "I am proud of your mother, Destiny." He leaned over and kissed the top of my head as he picked up my empty dinner plate and then headed toward the kitchen. "It took a lot of courage for her to extend an olive branch."

Once again, I tried to suppress my irritation that the first compliment Josh had given me in months was because I was nice to Ruthie.

"You could be a little more grateful and grace-filled, Destiny." I tried to be patient with my still-teenaged daughter. "I'm doing this for you. I'm trying to save your inheritance. I'm trying to do the right thing."

"Sounds to me like you're trying to avoid the consequences of not paying a living wage."

Wow. That was a zinger I hadn't expected. "You don't know even know what we pay Ruthie."

"Not enough for all she does for us. If you paid her better, she wouldn't be suing us."

There's not enough money in the world to put up with your smart mouth and entitled attitude, I want to spit back. "I'm not going to discuss the details of our finances with you, but our compensation for Ruthie's services has always been competitive with market rates." I was seething with rage.

Teenagers can be so infuriating. Destiny was the one who took Ruthie most for granted. I couldn't believe she was getting on her high horse and acting superior about this. And it hurt that she was siding with an employee over her own mother. Regardless of anything else, when it came down to it, Ruthie was paid to help, whereas I had *given* that girl everything.

"Whatever you have to tell yourself to sleep at night" Destiny had to put in one last punch.

More like whatever I have to do to keep from strangling my daughter! In this case, it's excusing myself from the table and taking the bottle of wine with me. I might circle back for the rest of the ice cream, too.

Stumbletrick,

Nice job following instructions. Apparently, we've found something you can do if I am explicit enough. Now for follow up. You can't just willy-nilly pull whatever you want out of your bag of tricks and throw it against the wall to see what sticks. This situation requires the skill and expertise of a surgeon like me, not the clumsy whacking of an amateur like yourself.

To prevent you from further messing up things beyond repair, I'll continue to make it simple enough even for you to follow along. *Keep her focused on herself*—her feelings, her efforts, even her flaws. My preference, of course, is to have her comfortably smug and basking in her superiority, but failing that we can work with a morbid fixation on her weaknesses. If she starts to veer into the dangerous territory of considering the feelings and perspectives of others, re-direct her immediately. That old but effective question, "I wonder what they think about you?" should do it.

Keeping it simple for you, stupid —

Twisttale

CHAPTER FIFTEEN

Guess Who's Coming to Dinner

ABBY'S JOURNAL

Saturday, February 20th —

OMG, what have I done? I can't do this. What was I thinking? My own daughter isn't on my side. My girlfriends aren't either. Eden thinks I should have listened to the attorney and, as he phrased it, stayed the hell away from Ruthie. Ivy has recently discovered everyone—especially me apparently—is racist. She suggested I attend an online diversity, equity, and inclusion (DEI) workshop before Friday. Even Jessica wondered if dinner was a good idea. "A couple of hours in the same room with someone attacking you? I'm willing to bet you'll say something you'll regret."

She's right. I have put my foot in my mouth in almost every possible opportunity since I was born. What made me think I could pull this off?

I will make it worse. I know I will. I always do. Maybe I should cancel. But then I would offend Ruthie all over again, and they will tell me how terrible I am for doing that. I can't win.

What has happened to me? I used to be brave. Or maybe I was just naïve. Regardless, when we were first married, I wasn't afraid to do the bold, daring thing. Marrying Josh, moving across the ocean, facing the unknown, trying new things, starting a new career—those things take courage. In fact, the surest way to get me to do something was to tell me I couldn't.

That deeply ingrained optimism sprang from the belief that Josh had my back. Together we could do anything. I always believed that if I did my best, surely everything would turn out the way it was supposed to.

It feels like the opposite now. Everyone criticizes, and everything falls to pieces no matter what I do. And instead of having my back, Josh sides with my detractors. He talks about loving other people and looking at things from their perspective, but why doesn't he ever look at things from mine?

The whole situation feels so hopeless. Why do I keep trying? It's so tempting to give up and let it all go to hell.

Dear Corel,

Remember what Our Lord told them? "In this world you will have trouble. But take heart! I have overcome the world." It breaks my heart to see our sweet girl falling for our fallen brothers' clever attacks, but we have every reason to hope even when things seem bleakest. It is true our enemies are bold and crafty. After all, their leader tried his tricks—quoting Scripture and twisting the truth—on Our Lord Himself when He walked the earth.

But Our Lord always shows us the way forward. We can find ways to prepare Abby's heart and mind for this dinner. Hope and beauty are our tools, not theirs. When the human heart responds to beauty in nature, design, art, music, literature—anything that awakens an awareness of good outside themselves—it is a step toward God.

The forces of evil try to twist the attraction of beauty into vanity, or lust, or materialism, or greed. But those distortions only prove its true power. So do not be deceived. Two things and two things only can pierce through the veil between this world and theirs: affliction and beauty. Affliction because it is an invitation to join in Our Lord's redemptive suffering. Beauty because it reveals the character of God.

Right now, Abby exaggerates Ruthie's negative qualities, so let's help her see the beauty of her darker-skinned sisters. Maybe introduce her to the lyrical simplicity and power of Maya Angelou's poetry. Or could you orchestrate an opportunity for her to see Maria Tallchief dance? Or simply bring to mind the warmth of Michelle Obama's ready smile.

We can't undo centuries of systematic programming by our enemy in an instant, but these small moments can start to melt its power. Chip away at the lie that the souls of her sisters and brothers shrouded in different-hued flesh are somehow less worthy than she is.

Help her see the beauty of diversity. Remind her that one child of God is never superior to another, but rather all are equally awe-inspiring—the raucous rolling rhythm of a gospel choir *and* the majestic, perfect synchronization of the Mormon Tabernacle Choir.

First, she must realize that she has believed a lie, and then she can take responsibility for internalizing it. One step at a time, dear warrior. Help her first to see the truth and then to embrace it.

For the Glory of Our Lord,

Ariam

ABBY'S JOURNAL

Wednesday, February 24th —

Am I doing the right thing? What is the right thing? What are my motivations? Am I an evil colonial racist capitalist oppressor trying to assuage guilt? I don't think so. But everyone seems eager to say that I am.

Regardless, the infamous dinner still needs to be prepared, so I went to the grocery store to get a nice cut of beef. That's one concrete thing I can do. While checking out, I noticed the old woman in line behind me. I know how to stretch a penny, so I recognize it when I see it. No one her age gets discount-brand frozen pizza and ramen by the case unless they have to.

I wanted to help, but I was afraid if I offended her, she might cause a scene. Who knew what kind of public tongue-lashing that shuffling little grandma in orthopedic shoes and support hose might be capable of? Still worse, someone could video it and the footage go viral, and I could become a white savior complex meme. Stranger things have happened these days.

I bagged my groceries as slowly as possible at the end of the checkout, waiting to see her total. When I knew I had enough cash to cover it, I leaned over and said just loudly enough that she wouldn't ask me to repeat it, "Ma'am, could I pay for your groceries?" as I handed her two folded bills.

She grabbed me with both arms, pulled me against her chest, and said more to the ceiling than to me, "The Lord must've told you I was in need!" She smelled like soap and felt like the softest pillow.

It was the absolute last thing I'd expected. Embarrassed but relieved, I made a hasty exit, still afraid to look her in the eye. That was the best $40 I've ever spent.

Dear Corel,

Two birds with one stone—well done!

You saw the opening and took it—inserting yourself between our girl and her tormentor. I saw you block that thought about "forty dollars won't change anything" and then deflect the arrow about "better to just mind your own business." Our enemies try to minimize the power of small deeds, but *every* act of love is a celebration of our Creator.

In addition to helping her expand her understanding of justice toward her neighbor, you also tore a hole in another lie—the sinister deception that pervades Abby's world without her realizing it. Although it seeps into almost everything she does, if she were to speak the lie out loud and expose it to the light of truth, she would see it for the fraud that it is.

I'm talking about that idea that the chief end of man is the accumulation of material goods and comfort. If you spelled it out like that, she would object, yet it determines how she weighs every decision.

Today, you gave her a glimpse of the joy of giving. A mere taste, perhaps, but that's how we operate. The demons and demagogues move masses. That is not our way. We speak to the heart. Keep encouraging small acts of kindness wherever you can. Like a tiny sprinkle of salt adds flavor or a single flame can light up the darkness, so does a sliver of love bring real change to the human heart.

I thank Our Father above, dear Corel, for using your courage, wisdom, and strength to strike this crucial blow against our enemy's web today. May He continue to lead and guide you.

For His Kingdom and Glory,

Ariam

Dear Coward,

You lost us significant ground today. I can now add spinelessness to your growing list of failings. I'm not interested in excuses or complaints about how you were sucker punched by a Guardian at the grocery store. Opposition comes with the territory. Better get used to it.

Someone must be praying for this vile creature. But at least we know our enemy by sight now. A hulking brute, you say? Strong enough to take on a dozen devils at once? I wonder why our Enemy would assign a powerful foe to a pitiful case like this. A clever Guardian, too, to bring that old woman into the mix.

No matter. He knows what you look like as well—along with how you ran away like a scared cockroach at the first threat of violence, which undoubtedly will only increase his boldness. He probably doesn't realize the head of the North American division is also working this case. Perhaps we'll let him build up false confidence a little more to counteract the damage done by your cowardice and stupidity. All the better for a surprise attack later.

Your ineptitude no longer surprises me —

TwistTale

PS - Don't think I won't be writing you up for this just because I can't be bothered to berate you sufficiently in this missive. Our superiors will mete out your punishment soon enough.

ABBY'S JOURNAL

Thursday, February 25th —

Children can be such a blessing. Not always, mind you, as my exchange with Destiny over dinner last week reminded me. I was almost ready to give up on them. I love them to death, of course. I would—and have—sacrificed everything for them, but Destiny can be a pill, and most of the time Cash goes off and does his own thing without a word or thought about his mom.

But today, they were there for me. Maybe they've noticed how the lawsuit and all the conflicts were wearing on me. Or maybe they've noticed that I was late with their tuition checks. Regardless of what inspired it, Cash texted me: "I'm glad you're my mom." And Destiny uttered six words I never thought I'd hear her say, "What can I do to help?"

Be still my heart. Sweet precious girl. My adorable boy. They are both so beautiful and pure. It makes my blood boil that back-stabbing Ruthie wants to cheat you out of your inheritance even if you don't know enough to recognize it. Don't worry, sweethearts. Mama bear will fight for you.

Stumbletrick,

I didn't think you had it in you. The way you deflected that Guardian's pathetic effort to inspire her children to show their mother a little love and then transformed it into self-righteous indignation on her part reminded me of something I would do. My instruction must finally be breaking through that thick skull of yours.

Isn't it astonishing the kind of moral pretzels pride and haughtiness make possible? "I'm such a good, loving person that I will hate for you." Ha! It's hilarious.

But it takes more than one lucky shot to win the game. Let's see if that move was just a fluke and you're back to your infantile attempts at manipulation. Tomorrow's the big night. Try to keep it going.

My money's on fluke—

Twisttale

P.S. – I'm contacting Muddleweb as well and informing him of our latest intel. He probably doesn't know Our Enemy has brought in the big guns in this case. We can't afford to let them get the advantage over you.

ABBY'S JOURNAL

Friday, February 26th —

I can't believe the dinner is tonight. I'm so nervous I've stress-eaten my way through a package of Oreos. Now I feel sick on top of everything else. I don't know what I was thinking when I decided to make it all from scratch. Every time I threw out a potential menu idea, Josh told me it didn't matter what we ate. Men—I wish they'd keep their noses out of what they don't understand. Of course, it matters! Setting a bunch of Styrofoam take-out containers on the table does not communicate the same thing as a home-cooked meal. Next, he'll be telling me it doesn't matter what I wear. The billion-dollar fashion industry says differently.

I think I may have overdone it on the meal plan, though, just to prove him wrong. Tonight was probably not the best night to try beef wellington for the first time. I do think it shows effort, however. No one can say that I'm not treating Ruthie like an honored guest. I never claimed to be a master chef. Heck, that was one of the reasons I needed Ruthie's help in the first place. I'm going to call it a win if dinner is edible.

Plus, culinary gymnastics will keep me from thinking too much. Even though I know that I have not been completely fair to Ruthie, thinking about the lawsuit still makes me angry. What did my life coach say? I am entitled to be upset. Damn straight, I am.

I am entitled to be upset when someone attacks me, my home, and my children's future. I am entitled to be upset when a person I trusted turns against me and puts a knife to my throat. I am entitled to be upset when the person who rocked my babies leaves them to blow in the wind.

But being upset is not going to help. Tonight, I am going to try to listen. Tonight, I'm going to let Josh take the lead. Tonight, I am going to try my hardest not to be defensive or aggressive. Lord, please help me.

Saturday, February 27th —

So that didn't work.

I tried. I really did. But I always manage to say the wrong thing, and Ruthie has a talent for getting under my skin—not a great combination. I can't stop putting my foot in my mouth, and she can't keep her smart mouth shut.

It started out okay. "Hi, Ruthie! Come in. We're so glad you came." But after only two sentences, I felt an unexplainable need to fill the awkward silence and added, "Love what you're trying to do with your hair!"

As soon as I said it, the words tasted sour in my mouth. Ruthie, who had been taking off her coat, paused and said, "So glad you approve."

So that was the way we were going to play this. Believe it or not, it went downhill from there.

"Josh! Ruthie's here!" I called wearing a fake smile frozen on my face, internally reminding myself, *"Love your enemies. Do good to those who hate you."*

Josh came downstairs beaming. He hugged her like a long-lost best friend instead of the woman trying to bankrupt his children.

"Ruthie, so good to see you! How are you?"

"Oh, as well as can be expected. It's been a struggle, as you can imagine."

"Please tell me about it," Josh said ushering her to a comfy chair. I excused myself to finish up dinner and let them chat. That's why he was here, right? So he could do the stuff he is better at than I am, like showing empathy.

"Dinner's ready!" I announced when I put the final touches on the table.

Josh and Ruthie continued their cozy banter as they made their way into the dining room.

But at the door, Ruthie surveyed the table where she had served hundreds of meals before but never eaten as a guest. She eyed the brown mass on the silver platter suspiciously.

"What's that?"

"Beef wellington."

"I would have never guessed."

I bit my tongue, and we all sat. I bowed my head to indicate it was time for the blessing. I didn't hear a word Josh prayed, though. I was so busy trying to control my temper. Why did she irritate me so? I was trying to be open-minded, but every word out of her mouth felt like a put-down, like she was sizing me up, looking for any opportunity to take a jab, and then writing me off as irrelevant. She's always been that way. If I'd ask her to sew on a button, she'd suggest limiting myself to one piece of pie after dinner. If I asked her to pick up one of the kids, she'd quiz me on what I was doing instead. It's not my imagination. For years, I've honestly thought she often tried *not* to help me. I realize now that my own attitude might have contributed to that, but it's still a problem, considering that's what she was paid to do.

Suing us just confirms my suspicions.

As Josh finished his prayer, I told myself, *"Be charitable. Remember that she's just jealous and resentful because we have so much and she doesn't. Let her throw her jabs and nurse her resentments. You can rise above it."*

I remained silent while she and Josh chatted on and on, comfy and cozy as could be. When I stood to get the dessert, Ruthie said, "I know a girl who could let that dress out for you if you need one."

I pressed my lips together and tried to smile. "I miss having you around to help me with things like that."

"You know what I miss most, Ruthie?" Josh asked. His eyes lit up as they haven't for me in quite a while. "I miss your singing. I loved hearing you sing while you were cooking in the kitchen."

"I didn't realize you were listening." Ruthie laughed. "When the kids were little, songs were a great way to teach *and* distract them. Then I guess I never stopped."

After she and Josh continued their walk down memory lane for a while, Ruthie observed, "You've hardly said a thing since we sat down, Abby. Congratulations on keeping your promise to try to listen instead of talk. Might be a record for you."

How was I supposed to respond to *that*? How is a person supposed to take disrespect at her own table? I looked to Josh for help. He looked straight back into my eyes. But he said nothing. Leaving me to find the right thing to say.

Once again, I had done my best. I'd apologized. I'd invited her into my home, cooked the fanciest thing I could, showed her all the respect I could muster, and served her while she and my husband jawed on in a private little love fest. And yet, this was what I got—her backhanded compliments, her barely-veiled disdain. What does she want me to do? I can't change the past. Back in the day, I would just ignore her and her snide comments. They were all she had, after all.

But now, she had me by the throat.

If Josh wasn't going to defend me, I had no choice but to defend myself, "It seems you're not happy no matter what I do, Ruthie."

I wanted to say more, but I stopped myself. I wanted to kick her out. I wanted to scream at her that she's sitting at *my* table, eating *my* food, that I had given her a job that put food on her table for years, that the least she could do was show a little respect and gratitude.

But none of those words came out of my mouth before Ruthie shot back, "No, I'm not happy." Anger that had obviously been building for a while infused her voice. "I'm not happy that this is the first time in all these years you've invited me to sit at your table. I'm sorry if it puts a damper on your dinner party that I'm not going to pretend everything's fine and dandy because you said you're sorry for the first time in your life."

"I invited you here in good faith." I tried to keep my rising anger under control. "I was hoping this would go differently. Excuse me. You and Josh can finish dinner. Dessert is in the refrigerator."

I walked out of the dining room and straight through the front door. Upstairs wouldn't have been far enough. I couldn't get far enough away from her. If I stayed at the table much longer, I was going to slap her sassy mouth. Outside, I took a lap around the block to cool down, but then snuck back into our garage as the street was too public. There in the darkness, I beat my fists against the concrete in frustration and let the hot tears flow.

So no, the dinner idea didn't work.

Stumbletrick,

Don't exaggerate. "Epic triumph" seems a little overstated. We managed to take an impending disaster and pull out a victory of sorts, but you overestimate your success and the stakes. Yes, one dinner could have undone all our efforts and that was avoided. A single incident can destroy all our work—one glimpse behind the veil, one sinner's prayer, or one heartfelt word of repentance—and Our Divine Enemy could swoop in and wrench a victim from our clutches like Paul on the Damascus Road. Our Enemy calls it grace. I call it cheating. Regardless, it rarely happens that way, and we can't let the exceptions govern our strategy. Our Divine Enemy has a ridiculously unfair advantage, but you fail to recognize ours.

Here's the reality: these roots of deception go down deep. We weave the most intricate web of lies. We build up the bitterest resentment. We stoke the haughtiest pride. Someone (yours truly if you need it spelled out) scattered the seeds of racism, pride, materialism, and all the other things now proliferating in America. We've been planting, watering, and cultivating these insidious ideas for centuries. Chopping off the heads of these weeds won't do a bit of good. They will only grow back stronger.

In fact, let them cut! Cut them all down indiscriminately! I relish the chaos, the desperation. Let her try to take care of this pestilence on her own. It only spreads the seeds and makes it harder to distinguish between the wheat and the tares. In the meantime, keep telling her what a lovely lush field of weeds she has. I don't know how many times or different ways I can say it. Invisibility. Subterfuge. Deception. It is the path to success in America. What is more dangerous than an enemy you can't see?

That human vermin wants to believe so badly in her innocence that she will swallow any lie you tell her as long as she comes out looking and feeling vindicated. So keep telling her what she wants to hear: she's the good guy (or the victim, I don't care) and anyone who doesn't agree is the villain.

She doesn't know how to face her sin honestly, so she's got to lay the blame somewhere.

In the meantime ... do I have to point out every little thing to you? Don't forget our primary target. After that performance at dinner, you've got a fresh opportunity to leverage the hell out of that growing divide between her and her husband.

Don't waste it —

Twisttale

ABBY'S JOURNAL

Sunday, February 28th —

After dinner on Friday night, Josh came looking for me. I heard him in the backyard calling, "Abby, where are you?" but I stayed silent. I wasn't ready to be found.

The worst part about that entire dinner fiasco was not Ruthie's snark. What else would I expect? It's no secret she's mad at me.

It was also not the fact that she was right—about my dress, about my comment on her hair, about the beef. I have gained weight (no thanks to her and the stress she's put me through). I do put my foot in my mouth. I was trying to show off. I shouldn't have attempted such an ambitious recipe.

The worst part was Josh not standing up for me. Nothing at all. I thought we would present a united front. I thought he would stand by my side and help Ruthie to understand our perspective. Instead, he treated her like a returning hero and left me dangling in the wind.

Who does that? Who throws their wife to the lions to be devoured? Worse, who invites the lions in, tickles their ears, and then smiles as they attack? He might have defended me or fought for us both, if not for my sake, then at least for the children. I don't know how to live with a man who won't fight to protect his family.

And by the way, why does he get a pass? Why is she all chatty with him but mad at me? I don't recall him inviting her for dinner in the dining room. So what if he suggested that early on and I shot him down, saying we didn't want to start a precedent? She doesn't know that.

Regardless, I didn't answer when he called my name. I didn't want to talk to him. I'm not sure I want to be married to him.

Dear Corel,

We can't lose heart. Deep inside—under her defensiveness, pride, and self-centeredness—she bears the divine image of God. Hold on. Don't let go.

This is the work: sanctification. It's not easy—not for her and not for us. But our Lord has paved the way. He has won the ultimate victory over sin and death. His sacrifice turned the tide, and our triumph is assured, but we must continue this trench warfare to save as many souls as possible until the final battle.

No matter how deceived she is, how far gone she may seem, or how deeply rooted her blindness or her sin, Our Lord sees her and loves her as His beloved child.

We must help Abby to see her true enemy. It is not Ruthie or her husband. But learning requires humility, which is why our enemies discourage it ardently and why Our Lord lists pride as the thing he hates most. I know we can do it, Corel. I know our girl has it in her. Our enemies may pull the cords of deception tight around her heart, but the sword of truth can cut her free. Stay the course. We will overcome.

For His Glory,

Ariam

CHAPTER SIXTEEN

A Place of Power

ABBY'S JOURNAL

Tuesday, March 2nd —

I had an emergency phone session with my life coach last night. I missed all our appointments last month. First, I was busy with house shopping. Then I couldn't get out of bed because I was so conflicted about helping Jessica. (I still don't know what she decided to do.) Then came the lawsuit, the dinner, and that whole mess. I also kept getting these terrible headaches before each appointment. With so much on my plate right now, though, I can't wait any longer to talk to someone objective.

After I told her the basics, it only took one "How does that make you feel?" for me to vomit all my angst—about Josh, his judgement, my fears that he doesn't even like me anymore, and most of all his betrayal.

"Have you considered talking with Josh about it? Do you think that would make you feel better?" Absolutely not. Therapists ask the silliest questions sometimes.

What would make me feel better? Forgiveness. Unconditional love. If only they weren't unrealistic pipe dreams.

Actually, Josh is good at forgiveness. He's not one of those people who keeps a scorecard or brings up old grievances and throws them in your face. He's forgiven me so many times over the years—for being self-centered and lazy, yelling at the kids, eating all the ice cream, monopolizing the conversation, neglecting him. There's no way I could remember them all. But those were little things.

Do you want to know something crazy? Sometimes when I'd ask his forgiveness for something I'd done, I'd slide down and sit at his feet. Not always. But sometimes. I can see Ivy hyperventilating at the mere thought. It's weird, I know, and I certainly haven't told anybody else that. But when

I wronged him, when I needed him to understand that I knew what I'd done, it seemed like the only way. The natural thing, even. I wanted to be close to him.

It's kind of like that old Aesop's fable about the wind and the sun making a wager about who could get the man to take off his coat. If Josh had tried to force me or in the slightest way implied that I should kneel, I would have been gone as fast as if he'd suggested we buy a timeshare. The fact that he would never force me to do something like that is part of what made me want to.

I've got a rebellious streak a mile wide and twice as long. I don't like to be told what to do. Growing up, I never wore my seatbelt. Even though I knew it was the smart choice, everyone trying to make me wear it only encouraged my determination not to. It was my choice, after all. I'm not hurting anyone. What right do others have to tell me what to do with my own life?

But one day, Josh turned to me while we were in the car. He looked me straight in the eye and asked, "What can I do to get you to wear your seatbelt?" I couldn't have told him, but as soon as that simple question left his mouth, I clicked it on. He's always been my sun, making me want to shed my coat while the rest of the world played the wind trying to blow it off my back.

But that's changed. He doesn't feel like my warm, loving, forgiving husband anymore. He feels like a judge on a high seat, looking down on me, willing me to be something other than who I am. Just because he doesn't scold doesn't mean he doesn't secretly think less of me. How could he help it?

And it would be worse if he knew *everything*.

I try not to think about that. If I were in a movie (and Catholic), perhaps I could drive to a town where no one has ever met me, admit my sins to a priest behind a screen, do my penance, and move on. But a life coach can't give absolution, so I'm not going to confess. It can't be undone. Try to forget, press forward, and do better next time ... like in helping Jessica.

The past can't be undone. Best to leave it alone.

Stumbletrick,

What a delightfully ghastly report! Exactly what I like to see: the victim is trapped. She's seeking an escape from guilt for a sin she's not even willing to admit or name, and so desperate she'd do almost anything—except the one thing that could cure it—repentance. Perfect.

As usual, this has little to do with you and everything to do with the excellent work of your predecessors (like me). If there was a hologram of a fire-breathing dragon or a blood-thirsty clown in front of the confession booth, she couldn't be more terrified of exposure. The idea of having to look another human in the eye, admit her fault, her grievous fault, and ask for forgiveness is unfathomable for her. So we're safe ... for now.

But I don't believe in taking chances. Don't rely on her fear alone to keep her from confession and repentance. Send her off in another direction in that maze of guilt. Plant a giant hedge in front of the exit. Add some thorny rose bushes. Or a fake wall. Put a puppy at the end of the path, so she walks right past the opening. You get the point.

You know I'm not a fan of the life coach, but since you can't seem to eliminate the annoying pest, at least use her to lead your victim around in circles. Remember, the coach doesn't have to be complicit in the ruse. She can't provide a cure if our victim won't share her disease. The coach will think she's helping by encouraging the human to find the answers inside herself, or better yet, by blaming others. Delicious.

Did I use small enough words for you this time, you idiot?

Try to keep up —

Twisttale

Dearest Corel,

I love your warrior heart!

I know you want to swoop down, gather her in your arms, and carry her to a place of safety. Indeed, we must get her to a place of strength and refuge, but the path to healing often hurts along the way.

Mother Teresa explained it so beautifully:

> Anyone who imitates Jesus to the full must also share in his passion [crucifixion]. We [humans] must have the courage to pray to have the courage to accept. Because we do not pray enough, we see only the human part. We don't see the divine, and we resent it. I think that much of the misunderstanding of suffering today comes from that from resentment and bitterness. Bitterness is an infectious disease, a cancer, an anger hidden inside. Suffering is meant to purify, to sanctify, to make us Christlike.

See? It *is* possible. A few of them get it. Strangely enough, it's usually the humans who lean into suffering while on earth, like this tiny precious nun who comforted India's poor and dying. The ones tripped up by esoteric questions like the problem of pain tend to be the ones who are sheltered from life's worst struggles. I think they have more time to listen to our enemies' lies and less opportunity to experience God's grace.

Our enemies tell them that their suffering means that Our Lord must not care. What an outrageous lie! It's the exact opposite. Did He not love His own Son? Did His own Son not suffer?

Indulgence and comfort do not strong bodies or hearts make. Our Heavenly Father wants their very best. He can redeem their pain and use it to draw them back to Himself—with greater appreciation for His redemptive love in the process.

So, Corel, our objective has never been to cease her suffering. In some cases, we might need to let it unfold despite our desire to comfort her. In fact, we might not understand it until the very end.

But we know that Our Lord can redeem every bit of it. We know that if she offers up her suffering to Him, it can be purifying and beautiful and transform her into Christ's likeness.

But if she does not, the bitterness and resentment will eat her alive.

Oh, how we long for her to turn and find grace and help!

Godspeed, dear warrior, fight on for the love of our girl and for the glory of our Great Redeemer,

Ariam

ABBY'S JOURNAL

Sunday, March 7th —

Where do I start? First, I can't believe I ran out of gas on the way to church. I filled up not that long ago. Maybe someone siphoned fuel from my tank like in the movies. And of course, it would happen on the one morning Josh is out of town and I was experimenting with a new route.

Roadside assistance said they couldn't be there for at least an hour. Fortunately, I had stalled right in front of an old rundown redbrick church. Through the open stained-glass windows, I could hear the familiar notes of an old hymn, and the church van parked inside a chain-link cage topped with curled barbed wire made me think maybe I'd be safer not waiting in my stalled car.

There couldn't have been more than a few dozen people scattered throughout the sanctuary, all facing a gray-haired woman pounding on a rickety piano and a balding preacher with a surprisingly clear tenor voice. I slid into a back pew, joined the last verse of Amazing Grace, and hoped my presence wouldn't draw too much attention.

No chance. The scrawny-looking preacher welcomed me from the pulpit first thing, and I anticipated the parishioners descending on me like a long-lost grandchild at the end of the service.

The sermon was not impressive. *My* pastor has a delivery so smooth he could have a second career doing movie trailer voiceovers. Every Sunday, he whips out carefully crafted alliterations and thought-provoking zingers with dramatic flair.

This little guy was in sad need of a Toastmasters class and kept harping on tired old phrases like repentance for sins, being filled with the Holy Spirit, and on fire for the Lord. I found myself wondering how many times these people have sat through essentially the same sermon.

I haven't gotten to the weird part, though.

I wasn't the only visitor. Another apparent stranger, probably homeless, possibly high, entered the church as well. A short-haired brunette in leather pants, she smelled of urine when she passed me. She strode right up the center aisle in the middle of the sermon, re-arranged the candles, and then knelt at the altar. She lifted her hands in the air, muttering some unintelligible gibberish. Like any rational person, I was terrified of what she might do next.

I expected an usher or the pastor to do something. Maybe strongarm her and guide her out the back door? But no one did. Instead, an ancient-looking woman with white hair hobbled up, placed her hands on the woman's shoulders, and softly sang the words of that old blessing, "The Lord bless and keep you...."

The woman in leather started sobbing. Several men rose from their seats. I thought, *Okay, now they'll escort her out.* But they joined in the craziness—some praying, some singing, some adding their hands on her back. No one broke up the outlandish display and brought the service back to order. I guess the good news was that all eyes were on *her*, not me, as I slipped out to meet the guy with the gasoline.

I didn't emerge completely unscathed, though. I had pushed open the dark wooden door and thought I escaped into the cool air and sunlight when a stray parishioner's voice caught me. "We're so glad you came to visit today. Before you go, is there anything I can pray about for you?"

My first thought was that I should be praying for *them* considering their lackluster pastor and troublesome guests. But I'd probably never see this person again, and I could definitely use some prayer. I faced her and smiled. "Sure. Could you pray that I would learn to love Ruthie?"

That wasn't what I had meant to say. My words shocked me. It would have made sense to ask for prayer for Josh, for our marriage, or for the lawsuit—all of which I'd considered mentioning. Instead, I found myself standing on a church stoop with a stranger, our heads bowed, her hands on my arms, listening to her ask the Lord to soften my heart toward Ruthie, to help me see her the way God sees her. And then I voiced a surprisingly not-insincere, "Amen." Although, when it was my turn to pray, I did throw in a last-second request that the lawsuit be resolved favorably, too.

Stumbletrick,

Where do I start—with your incompetence, your ignorance, or your reckless stupidity? My expectations were so low that I honestly didn't think you could disappoint me further, but here we are.

Perhaps most concerning of all is your failure, even now, to see the severity of your blunders. If my minions and I hadn't already advanced this case almost past the point of redemption, this mistake could have been fatal.

First, you demonstrate a severe lack of judgment by viewing your *victim's* church—our playground—as a threat. Then, you err on the other side by allowing your victim to waltz into a veritable fortress. Perhaps you were all puffed up because you evaporated the gas in her car, but then you let her stop right in front of that church! You were surprised that you couldn't get in? That a Guardian bound you when you tried to pull her away from that meddling old biddy? I would think you would be more familiar with overt spiritual warfare from your experience in the East.

I can't believe you didn't recognize it. What did you think they were doing in there? Playing bridge? Don't start with the blame game. There are any number of things you could have done to prevent her from walking through those doors. How about a handsome stranger on a motorcycle offering to give her a ride to the closest gas station? Could have been two birds with one stone, you idiot.

But instead, we have an unmitigated disaster. You don't even realize the damage you've done, the forces you've unleashed. I'm not saying we won't still prevail, but you've just made my job a lot harder.

Thanks a lot, you moron —

Twisttale

Dear Corel,

Bravo, warrior! I'm raising my glass with a few other angels, toasting your victory and wishing you continued success. The road is long. Let's savor the milestones along the way.

Thank you for your report, but of course, we were already celebrating from the moment we heard the prayers in that beautiful church—sweet music to our ears, the petitions and praises of God's children.

Tell me, did you orchestrate the appearance of the stranger as well or just the empty gas tank? I don't need to know the details, but they are so fun. Of all the wonderful things accomplished on that glorious Sunday morning, I'm most excited that you have enlisted another prayer warrior on Abby's behalf!

A full-grown lion can fight off a single predator or even many predators, but relentless attacks by dozens of hyenas can kill even the king of beasts. But when another lion joins the fight, however, it completely changes the dynamic. Two fighting together are exponentially more powerful than either one alone. So we rejoice that Abby now has multiple warriors fighting on her side!

And that's just the beginning. I'd wager the sword of truth has made more than a few strategic cuts in that web of deceit that has our girl in such a stranglehold. Well done, my dear friend. Well done.

With admiration for you and joy in Our Lord,

Ariam

CHAPTER SEVENTEEN

Take Me to Church

ABBY'S JOURNAL

Tuesday, March 9th —

I keep thinking about that smelly brunette at the church. Why didn't they throw her out? I would have. Of course, I would have done it nicely— maybe even given her a bus pass and card with the address of a rescue mission or something. But they weren't merely polite. They embraced her and sang blessings over her. Who does that?

Wednesday, March 10th —

I told my life coach about my adventure. Well, I told her about the little church, the strange woman, and how they gathered around her. I left out the part about praying for my relationship with Ruthie. I know we're supposed to love everyone. I didn't realize until I asked that woman to pray for me that I don't really love Ruthie. Lord, please help me! I can't do this on my own.

Thursday, March 11th —

Josh is still out of town, so I went back to that little church last night. I'm not sure why. It felt like something was guiding me back there even though normally it would be the last place I would go.

I figured a place like that would meet for a midweek service. I wasn't wrong. I came late, sat in the back, and listened. I didn't know what I was hoping for, but I wasn't disappointed. I got more of the same as Sunday— even less production value and even more dysfunction.

In the open-mic sharing time after the Bible study, a skinny unshaven man stood in the back rambling on and on while I wondered who would intervene. It was time for an artful political handler to liberate the microphone from his grasp. They need to train someone to deal with these situations.

After he finished, a pretty young blond shared painful details of her divorce like she was updating girlfriends over wine instead of standing in front of dozens of people. Did no one ever teach her to filter?

I, of course, said nothing. This church was a place for broken people. I don't consider myself a broken person. But it's kind of nice that there's a place where it's okay not to be perfect. It's okay for a grown man, probably drunk, to stand and cry as he talks about how he has disappointed his kids. It's okay for the now-single mom to divulge her struggles with resentment toward the husband who left her. No one, except me, seemed to be judging them. I didn't know a place like that existed.

Friday, March 12th —

Until tonight, Josh and I hadn't talked about the Ruthie situation since the infamous dinner, partially because he left town for work shortly afterwards and was just now getting back. Secretly grateful to have the house to myself for a few days to clear my head, I hadn't even asked where he went.

I had dug out my now-long-abandoned happiness project and re-read my commandments. *Pay attention to what I pay attention to. Act the way I want to feel. Remember things that bring me joy. Connect meaningfully with others.* There were still three weeks until Easter. Better late than never.

Starting with commandment #2, I pretended everything was fine. I can be pretty good at conflict avoidance—metaphorically shutting my eyes and ears. *La-la-la. I can't hear you. If I can't see you, it's not happening.* So when Josh came home, I skipped right over everything else and told him about the little church.

Of course, Mr. Perfect already knew all about it. "I love it there," he said. "My dad does, too."

"Your dad—the man with more money than God—likes to go to a rundown building with stained ceiling tiles, listen to a one-note preacher, and rub elbows with the dregs of society? Somehow, I find that hard to believe."

"That's pretty harsh, Abby."

"You know what I mean." By the look on Josh's face, I knew I'd disappointed him—again. I backpedaled. "I'm just surprised. I didn't think that would be his cup of tea. Of course, your dad is lovely. He's just such the aesthete, with his gardens and gorgeous house, I thought he would want to worship somewhere beautiful."

"He does." It sounded like Josh and his father thought the church of broken people fit the bill.

"I know what you're getting at." I rolled my eyes. "I know all people are beautiful. 'You've never met a mere mortal, only immortal horrors or everlasting splendors' and all that. It's just that sometimes it's hard to concentrate on the beauty when you're distracted by all the mortal ugliness."

"Right again, my girl." Josh smiled and tapped his nose. "But I think that you and Dad would disagree on which part is beautiful and which is distracting."

Those two—Josh is such a chip off the old block.

Now that I'm paying attention (commandment #1), I see it. Josh and his dad both have a thing for underdogs. They hate pretense and showmanship. They value authenticity and sincerity, insist on kindness and gentleness, and above all else, they prize genuine expressions of self-less love. By those criteria, I guess that old decaying building rivals Notre Dame.

Saturday, March 13th —

Okay, commandment #4, connect meaningfully with others. I went back to see Shirley today. I almost called one of the girls instead. I knew they'd take my side. It's girlfriend code. They can criticize my parenting decisions, weigh in on my latest diet, even disapprove of my handling of Ruthie and the lawsuit. Oh, and they will absolutely judge me for my shoe choices. But I don't care if Josh and I disagreed about whether the world was flat or not, they would have my back. I can imagine Jessica's words now, *Girl, it's not about right or wrong. It's about being a partner. Did he even listen to you?*

But not Shirley. It seems she's always on Josh's side. She thinks he hangs the moon. She's been his number one fan since the beginning. So why did I go to see her?

Maybe because I know she'll tell me the truth. Right now, I need truth more than loyalty.

I sank into an overstuffed chair and spilled out my heart between sips of hot tea. She listened, nodded, and asked a few questions until, at last, I'd run out of words, having beaten the whole thing to death.

When I finished, Shirley cooed, "You know I love Josh, Abby."

"I know. I do, too. Maybe that's why I'm here—because I don't want someone else to trash-talk him. But I have to tell someone how I feel." Tears spilled down my cheeks.

"You can always come here, and I will always listen." She lifted the plate of snickerdoodles from the coffee table. "Would you like some more cookies?" I took another. "But now it's out, and it's not going to help to keep going over and over it."

"I only told you once."

"But how many times have you told it to yourself?"

Hmm, now that I'm paying attention—only every other waking thought for the last couple of months.

"What do you suggest instead?" I asked. I was pretty sure I wouldn't like the answer, but I need to move past this, so I'm currently accepting all suggestions on how.

"You go home and talk to him."

"But what about all the stuff I just told you? How he's taking Ruthie's side, and he's so judgmental, and how he doesn't do anything that shows me he loves me, and that he probably doesn't even like me anymore, and how he's not sticking up for me and the kids. Don't you think I have some valid points?"

"Not really," Shirley smiled mischievously as she reached out and put her hand on mine. "You know I love you, sweet girl, but marriage isn't about scoring points. It's about commitment and trust. That boy is the best thing that ever happened to you. Nine times out of ten, whether you think you are right or not, if you go home and do your best to love him, everything will be okay."

I sighed. "Well, you're certainly not a women's libber, Shirley."

"I'd give the same advice to a man. Go home. You've told it all to me. You've gotten it off your chest. You don't need to rehash it with every Jess, Eden, and Ivy." She winked. "Just leave it here, go home, and keep doing the things you know you're supposed to do."

"Okay." I got up to leave and wrapped my arms around her, "I love you, my friend, even if I don't always love the things you say."

Tough love is a steep price to pay for cookies, hugs, and a listening ear.

Stumbletrick,

I'm not interested in your excuses. Letting her go to Shirley's house again was a major mistake. You can't even go near that house yourself, so why did you think you should let her walk right in!

These missteps are serious. Do you see what is happening? She and her husband are talking. Next thing you know, they'll be laughing. She is praying and going to church—a real church, not a social club with a cross in front. And now she's going *back* to Shirley?

What are you waiting for? To throw them a shower at their vow renewal ceremony? I swear, you're going to roast over a spit before this is done. But I have no plans to join you. I am going to take over personally for the rest of the weekend. Your task is to keep her away from that blasted little church for a mere twenty-four hours while I save at least one of our wart-covered skins.

Think you can manage that, moron?

Twisttale

ABBY'S JOURNAL

Sunday, March 14th —

It felt so good to be back in our home church this morning—in our regular pew, singing songs I know, surrounded by smiling friends and even the twins as they are home for spring break. There was no danger of crazy homeless people, over-sharing alcoholics, or strangers asking me if they can pray for me.

I was so excited when I saw the sermon topic printed in the bulletin, "Why Bad Things Happen to Good People." Yes! Why are all these bad things happening to me? I'm a good person. Why are we getting sued? Why can't Josh love me for who I am? Why did my friend have to get pregnant? I couldn't wait to hear the answers.

Sitting on the edge of the pew, I listened. My pen poised to take notes. The pastor chastised those who spout callous remarks like, "Everything happens for a reason," and he delivered, with perfect sympathetic pitch, tearful statements like, "A loving God doesn't want babies to die." About twenty minutes in, though, I looked down at an empty page. Despite all the pleasant-sounding platitudes, the pastor hadn't given me any answers.

At first, I was disappointed. Then out of the blue, an idea struck me. Why wasn't he citing any Bible verses? Then I realized he rarely ever quotes the Bible in his sermons. Huh, maybe I should talk to him about that. Perhaps I should schedule a meeting and confront him about the lack of Scripture in his sermons. That would take a lot of courage, but someone has to be bold. Maybe it should be me.

I started taking all kinds of notes about what I might say to the pastor, citing different examples. It would be challenging, but it feels so good to take a stand and be courageous. I can't wait to tell Josh and the kids.

Stumbletrick,

You're so dim that I'm sure you don't realize what a victory I just scored. Sit back on your haunches and take notes because I'm going to give you a play-by-play.

I know I make it look easy. It's kind of like a no-hitter in baseball. There doesn't seem to be a lot going on at the surface, but for those in the know, the tension is palpable.

First, the build-up. You have gotten so few victories in this case that I'm not going to apologize for taking my time to savor this one. While the ubiquitous proliferation of Christian congregations throughout the American landscape remains one of Heaven's great strongholds, I suspect you now realize that we have been partially successful in mitigating that threat. Attending a church in middle America on Sunday mornings now implies about the same amount of connection to community and faith as going out to eat at a restaurant on Saturday night. It means nothing spiritual for many of them.

In Europe, ornate cathedrals and local parishes mar the physical landscape but are primarily empty shells. In America, their church buildings might be downright ugly, but they are often filled to the brim on Sunday morning. That's why we attack them from within rather than trying to keep people out.

Back to your victim, I'm not afraid of her church. Of course, Our Divine Adversary could gain a foothold in any congregation, large or small, but I do love the anonymity of a mega-church. Humans were created to be in relationship with one another. The more we can isolate them, the better.

With just a little assistance from us, your victim could go to church every week for years without making a single meaningful connection with another human, let alone another believer. But it's best if she never realizes this fact. This weekend, I encouraged our target to exchange smiles and pleasantries as these give us cover. If she never spoke to another human at church, she might wake up to the fact that she has no real connection and then leave, but the small talk gives the illusion of friendship.

No need to worry about the sermons. Thankfully, many pastors especially in her particular denomination rarely mention the actual words of Our Divine Adversary and, therefore, fail to tap into that power. This omission is one of our strategic victories. We have convinced them that studying or quoting the words of the Enemy is old-fashioned or inaccessible. Many believe their own words or those of other humans are somehow superior. These pastors more often than not base their sermons on books, movies, or even sports analogies. Whatever passing Scripture reading the service may contain has little chance of sticking in your victim's mind, especially with all the other distractions within the service—let alone the onslaught of information and stimuli she will receive once she is back on her phone. Honestly, a scripture verse converted into a meme by one of her friends in her social media newsfeed could have more impact on your victim than a dry cursory reading in a church service.

That said, today was the perfect opportunity to use one of my favorite tricks of the trade. I like to call it, "Speaking the truth in love." It sounds Biblical, so the deceit is even richer. The words are indeed from the Bible, but there is practically no chance she will look it up and read its context. Ironically, the original use of this phrase advocates for unity and reminds them to "be kind and tenderhearted, forgiving one another"—a far cry from what I have in mind.

This ingenious technique of "speaking the truth in love" suggests to your victim that her role is that of a critic. It encourages her to approach everything with a critical eye, believing it is her duty to discern everyone else's shortcomings and point them out. In some cases, we might convince the victim to confront the perpetrators themselves. Sound familiar? You see where this is going now? This takes her as far away from humility and loving others as possible. And, oh, the snowball effect when she voices her observations to a few more congregants!

But even if she doesn't go to the other humans and tell them what they are doing wrong, we have already won! For when she is most precariously positioned to examine her own heart, to consider what service to others she might do, or be encouraged by Our Divine Adversary's message of unconditional love and grace, her preoccupation with critique blinds her to all of it.

Can you now see all the undercurrents hidden in those innocuous-looking notes on her bulletin? And the party's just getting started.

I've done more in 24 hours than you've done in two months —

TwistTale

Dear Corel,

I admit I was a little nervous. I knew how many years her pastor has grappled with this challenging issue of the problem of pain. His tender heart bleeds for hurting people cut by callous responses to their suffering from humans claiming to bear the mantle of Christ. He prayed and worked so hard on that sermon. I could immediately see how discouraging and disheartening Abby's comments would have been to him. The self-righteous pride started growing in her heart as soon as she turned her focus from trying to understand, love, and serve to formulating her critique.

But what a stroke of genius on your part! I love it. You took her self-righteous impulse and desire for accolades, whipped them around and smashed the whole thing to pieces! Encouraging her to voice her thoughts to Josh—brilliant! I also loved your swift deflective moves when the demons must have realized where the discussion was going and tried to distract her—first with Destiny's latest escapades and then blowing up her phone with texts. It's not easy to keep Abby's focus on anything these days. Well done! I am impressed, but not surprised by your wise assistance to our dear girl.

For His Glory,

Ariam

ABBY'S JOURNAL

Monday, March 15th —

Well, that didn't go the way I expected.

I thought Josh would be proud of me for being brave enough to confront the pastor. He's the one always insisting on how important it is to study the Bible. I thought we would finally be on the same side.

But no.

When I informed the family over dinner about my plan to meet with the pastor this week, Josh didn't object right away, and to his credit, he didn't challenge me directly in front of the kids. Instead, he told a story—about a Bible professor who knew more about the Old Testament than probably any pastor around.

"The professor told me that when he went to church, instead of examining every theological point for correctness or considering what historical details could have added context, he tried to discern what message God might have for him that morning."

I knew what he was getting at. I know he's right, too, but it doesn't make me feel any better. Every time I try to be good, he raises the bar a little higher. Why can't he just be my cheerleader and support me for once? Is that too much to ask?

CHAPTER EIGHTEEN

Girls Night Out

ABBY'S JOURNAL

Wednesday, March 17th —

Just when I think Josh can't surprise me anymore, he comes up with the craziest ideas. When we were getting ready for bed, he suggested that I invite Ruthie to go out with my girlfriends and me.

I can't think of a worse idea.

It would give her more ammunition, more things to be offended about, more ways to feel slighted. It's best to limit interaction with Ruthie, like the lawyer suggested.

But when I told him that, Josh said, "That would be true if we had the same goal as the lawyer."

"What do you mean?" I had a bad feeling about what Josh was saying. "Of course, we have the same goal—to protect ourselves. What other goal could there be?"

"Reconciliation."

Oh, Josh, ever the idealist, with his beautiful words and lofty goals. They sound nice in theory, but they fall to pieces in the real world. That's why he needs me, the practical one, to bring him back down to earth.

"We tried that—I went to her house, I said I was sorry, we invited her over for dinner. None of it worked."

"You're right. None of it worked," he conceded softly, his sad eyes looking into mine.

"So, what makes you think anything will?"

"Faith. Hope. Love. All three?" He smiled playfully.

I let him wrap his arms around me even as I protested, "I think we need to be realistic." But I can't remember the last time I felt like I could please him. I let my head fall against his chest. Maybe this could be a step back closer together. I didn't *want* to invite Ruthie out with my friends, but I knew I could.

She'll probably say no anyway.

Thursday, March 18th —

She probably only said yes because she sensed I wanted her to say no. If so, I should have tried that tactic years ago.

Crap. Now what do I do?

Should I ask the girls for advice? No, I can't be honest with them about how Ruthie gets under my skin. Better to make it seem like it's no big deal. I can't wait to see Ivy's face when I show up with Ruthie in tow. Ha! How's that for diversity, equity, and inclusion?

But I need to talk to someone to make sure I don't mess this up. Another repeat of the dinner party will get me in hot water with the lawyer, Ruthie, *and* Josh.

Dear Corel,

I love your enthusiasm, but no matter what the Greek myths say, you can't make a person love with an arrow to the heart any more than you can make them forget with a potion. There are no shortcuts on this path.

We're making good headway in helping Abby recognize her sin. Heaven knows it's no small feat to cut through the web of deception that disguises her sins as virtues.

Meeting with Ruthie and acknowledging Ruthie's self-worth was an amazing first step, but Abby has deeper work to do as well. She needs to grieve her sin and its ugliness. Intellectual recognition is not enough.

Our goal is repentance and transformation. Those things can't happen without genuine sorrow that comes from seeing the truth of her sin.

Regardless of the legal outcome—she could be exonerated or bankrupted—it will not be a win for us if she doesn't weep for the wrong she has done so that she can experience forgiveness and grace. Think of King David in Psalm 51. Tears in this life can show the way to joy in the next, and not simply tears of frustration for the mess she's in, but tears of regret for the error of her ways and the hurt she has caused. Only then will she discover the abundant love, joy, and grace that Our Lord desires for her.

We can't jump ahead of this step.

For His Glory,

Ariam

ABBY'S JOURNAL

Friday, March 19th —

I wish all my friends were as responsive as Shirley. She never fails to text back immediately. After five paragraphs of me giving her the nitty-gritty on the latest with Josh and Ruthie, his crazy suggestion, Ruthie's response, and my current predicament, she sent back one single word of advice:

Listen.

I texted my reply clandestinely while Josh, the kids and I all watched a show together. It's been nice to have the twins home this week for spring break, but it does make it harder to talk without being overheard (or judged).

I know. I'm so bad at that. How do I keep my mouth shut?

Try counting to 10 before you speak.

Okay, Shirley's second suggestion was more practical. I like practical.

What else?

Ask questions.

Good. Any more suggestions?

The last one's harder.

Don't keep me in suspense, I typed when she didn't continue at first.

Try to see things from her perspective.

I clicked off my phone. That's all the advice I can handle at the moment. She and Josh are so similar. I'm asking for survival tips, just trying to army crawl my way out of this mess, and they want me to stand up and run toward the explosion.

Stumbletrick:

Have you learned nothing? I had to interrupt my dinner of a very tasty social media influencer to respond because your latest report demonstrated such a fundamental misunderstanding of the forces at play in this situation.

Didn't you see my letter about the weeds?

I know I said you are on a need-to-know basis, but apparently you need to know quite a bit more to raise you above the level of imbecile.

These little vermin are not angels who we're trying to seduce. They are sinners and slaves who we are preventing from being rescued. All you have to do is maintain the status quo. They *want* to sin and rebel. It's in their nature, thanks to the excellent work of our boss in the Garden of Eden. If we do nothing, they will still gravitate toward sin like addicts. Each hit is its own reward. Sin is where they feel comfortable. They can't help it.

Our Divine Enemy has the hard job—trying to transform them into something they are not.

We're merely keeping them rolling down the path to Hell. But for good measure, we put up a few additional guard rails to make sure they don't veer off the track.

We know the power of sin. It is poison. It destroys. It corrupts. Think for a moment: how could we best infect a whole culture with this devastatingly destructive force? That's what I've done. I've convinced them their sin is not harmful at all. It's nourishing.

Can you guess? You've been on this continent a while now. Can you see the sins that they celebrate, that they gulp down like cherry Kool-Aid on a hot summer day? The ones they can't even imagine giving up because they are inextricably woven into who they believe themselves to be?

How about their pride? It's number one on Our Enemy Above's hit list, but I've succeeded in convincing them it's not a sin, but an aspiration! How many humans have you seen in your short time here who actually strive to be proud? They look at some achievement—something our Enemy did with a little bit of their own help—and they claim credit and feel proud. It cracks me up every time.

Or how about their rugged individualism, as they like to call it? Sometimes when I need a lift, I like to watch 4th of July sermons where pastors try to explain how "loving your neighbor as yourself" really means giving your neighbor the freedom to help themselves. Oh, it's so satisfying to see them walk out of church and stroll right by the needy in their neighborhoods without a second thought.

Proper terminology is critical. Do you like how I renamed greed "entrepreneurship" and "capitalism"? Our Enemy tells them He will reward hospitality to strangers, but Americans don't encourage their children to hand out water to the thirsty. No, they romanticize teaching their kids to monetize resources with a lemonade stand that only serves those who can pay.

So back to my last letter. They've let these innocuous-seeming weeds proliferate so long, overtaking everything else, that if they tear them out now, they fear there will be nothing left but a wasteland. They believe they have no choice but to cling to the weeds and keep calling them a lush green lawn.

That's America in general, but let's talk more about your victim. Remember how I told you to encourage haughtiness? It's her poison. You scoff because you're an idiot, as does she because she's human. But as a demon, you should know better. She doesn't think haughtiness is bad. She's not even convinced it's a sin at all—more like a character flaw. Of course, she thinks she's better than Ruthie. But she also thinks it's not such a big deal. Her sense of superiority won't let her admit she's the bad guy—the self-centered, arrogant bad guy. It's the ultimate catch-22.

Trust in the power of sin. It does what we say it does. It corrodes. It perverts. It entraps. The almost invisible droplets of a virus can eventually cause injury and death, sometimes even better than the teeth of a lion.

Do you get it now? The last thing you want is her digging at the roots of this carefully planted field. How hard is that? She's naturally lazy. Keep her focused on herself. Divide. Isolate. Keep her mowing and admiring her weed-infested lawn while the house implodes.

That goes for Ruthie, too, but Muddleweb will take care of that.

I am running out of patience having to explain these things to you —

TwistTale

ABBY'S JOURNAL

Sunday, March 21st —

Could have been worse.

I did get to see Ivy speechless for the first time, well, ever, when Ruthie and I arrived at the restaurant. For all her high and mighty blather about systemic racism and reparations, she sure didn't go out of her way to be friendly to Ruthie.

None of the girls did. They were polite, of course. But after the initial surprise and polite brief exchanges, they chatted and laughed amongst themselves but left me to entertain my guest.

The strangest thing happened. The hostess sat us at a corner booth way in the back, and even the lovely Jessica couldn't manage to get our waiter's attention. I know, lots of people can tell sadder stories than having trouble getting their drinks refilled. Eden resorted to buying champagne by the bottle, and Jessica sidled her way through the ogling crowd of men around the bar each time we needed another round.

Regardless, there was something about sitting side-by-side in the leather booth with Ruthie in the back of the restaurant with music blaring and the girls enthralled in their own conversation that made it a little easier to speak more plainly to her than it had been on her porch or in my dining room.

We chatted about the kids, the music, and the girls (since they weren't paying any attention to us anyway).

By my third drink, I confessed, "I honestly didn't think you would come. I'm glad you did."

Ruthie must have felt the same because she admitted, "I wasn't going to. Until Josh called me."

Now she had my full attention. I wasn't sure what I thought about my husband calling other women behind my back.

"Can I ask how that conversation went?" I asked hesitatingly.

"You can ask." She laughed. Then after taking a sip of her chocolate martini (it had been Jessica's turn to pick the round), she continued, "He asked me to forgive you."

"Forgive me? For what?" I was more surprised than offended.

"I guess for being yourself."

Once again, I struggled with how to respond, but I tried to remember Shirley's advice. After a full count of ten seconds, I ventured, "Anything specific? I do have a lot of annoying qualities to choose from."

"If I had to narrow it down to one," Ruthie raised her dark eyes to the ceiling as she contemplated. "I'd say ... your superior attitude."

I was grateful that the noisy bar kept me from feeling the need to fill the silence. I let her words sit between us. Avoiding Ruthie's eyes, I looked past my drink, suddenly very interested in the band.

I closed my eyes and leaned my head back. Of course, my natural inclination was to defend myself or deflect, but we were past that. The problem wasn't really my attitude. It wasn't an "air" I project or a perceived slight from a comment I might make that could be corrected by a DEI workshop. It was that I fundamentally believed I was superior. For the first time I could hear the ugliness of that thought. Intellectually, I knew it was the unforgivable sin. In a democratic society, we're all supposed to say we are equal. But we're not. Some people are obviously superior to others. Bill Gates and Mother Teresa are better people than Ted Bundy and Al Capone. Americans may deny it with their words, but they sure don't with their actions.

"Guilty," I whispered at last. The word felt strange in my mouth. But I figured there was no harm in admitting it here in a crowded bar, right?

"Yes, you are."

I glanced sideways at Ruthie, trying to gauge her reaction. with a feeling of sadness in my heart ... for myself. Neither of us said anything for several minutes. I was still trying to process what was happening. I hadn't yet quite figured it out when the waiter made a rare appearance in our vicinity. I tried unsuccessfully to flag him down.

"Does it bother you?" I asked her.

"Does what bother me?"

"Being treated like this." I waved to the waiter who'd obviously heard— and ignored—me. "We've been to this restaurant a zillion times, and I've never been seated in this back room before or gotten such poor service. Being with you is the only thing that's different tonight."

"You can't fight all the battles all time."

I didn't know what was wrong with me. Maybe it was the dim lighting, the loud music, the feeling of intimacy. Perhaps it was the alcohol. But I looked straight into her dark brown eyes and confronted the elephant sitting between us, "What made you think that the battle with me was worth fighting?"

The usually whip-smart, wise-cracking Ruthie pressed her lips together. She returned my gaze and said five words, "Maybe you should ask Josh."

Uh oh. What did that mean?

I couldn't bear to ask her to explain, and I didn't think she would even if I asked.

"I'm tired." I scooted to the end of the booth. "I'm going to go. Thanks for coming out tonight. Can you manage to get yourself home?"

"I always do." Ruthie gathered up her things. After saying goodbye to the girls, we made our way toward the door. I surprised even myself by keeping my mouth shut. I didn't feel like talking, and heaven knows that never happens.

We waited for our Uber rides in silence. As Ruthie climbed into hers, she dropped one more bomb, "If you and Josh would like to come to my church tomorrow, the service starts at 10:30." She got into the car before I could manage a response.

Stumbletrick,

Are you kidding me? I am still flabbergasted by how you have managed to mess up in a matter of weeks this shtick that has been working quite well for the last few hundred years. I can only imagine how a night out with those two might have played out only a few months ago. I'm seeing a possible catfight—slapped faces, pulled hair, screamed obscenities— definitely *not* an invitation to church. This whole thing is sliding into the crapper faster than Montezuma's revenge. All I can say is that you better make sure she doesn't go inside those church doors tomorrow morning ... or you will have Hell to pay.

Seething at your incompetence —

Twisttale

CHAPTER NINETEEN

Guess Who's Coming to Church

ABBY'S JOURNAL

Sunday, March 21ˢᵗ —

I probably should have driven. Or walked with Josh. But he left early in order to visit with people before the service started, and I didn't want to do that.

So I walked alone. With each step, I found myself longing more and more for the safe cocoon of rolled up windows when going through this neighborhood as well as a quick escape route when the service was over. I guess I thought our new Tesla would be a little conspicuous, but it couldn't have stood out more than I did in my dress and heels walking down the cracked sidewalk edged by chain-link fences and weedy lawns on the way to Ruthie's church.

I know everyone says it's impossible to understand the minority experience, but I think I got a taste today. I could feel the weight of the curious stares of the mostly unseen residents in the rundown houses and their unspoken question, "What the hell is *she* doing here?"

At least, that's what I assumed they were asking. I never normally go north of the railroad tracks, and now I've been here twice in the last few weeks. It's less than a mile from my own beloved quiet tree-covered boulevard, but a different world entirely. My anxiety was so high by the time I got to the old redbrick building I considered passing right by its propped open metal doors and continuing on toward the comforting white steeple of a Presbyterian church a few blocks away.

I approached the church from the opposite side of the street to give myself a chance to abort at the last moment if needed. As I drew nearer, I watched men in suits and freshly polished shoes and women in their Sunday best making their way inside the double doors. At the last possible minute, I held my breath and crossed the street. As I lifted my head to walk up the stairs, friendly eyes, wide smiles, and warm outstretched hands greeted me. Hearty "good mornings" filled my ears. Even though the service had not yet started, the sound of music and conversation coming from the sanctuary was louder than the full volume of the songs we sing at my regular church.

Josh was standing inside the sanctuary with Ruthie, comfortably chatting with her and a crowd of others. I came up beside him, and he put his arm around my waist and smiled down at me. I tilted my head against his shoulder for a moment, and my breath came a little easier.

"Thank you for inviting us, Ruthie." My gratitude for the invitation was sincere, even if accepting it was difficult.

She was too busy holding court to give me more than a nod and a pleasant smile of acknowledgment. That's okay. For once, I didn't want any additional attention.

I would have preferred a seat in the back, but Josh led me to a crowded pew toward the front. Always a little rhythm-challenged, I ignored the admonition to "put your hands together" as the worship began, but Josh joined right in.

The service was a little loud and a lot long for my taste. When the bells from the other nearby churches sounded noon and things showed no signs of slowing down, I was glad we had let the kids stay home in bed. Ruthie might have heard my stomach growling because she discreetly passed me a bag of goldfish, which I accepted with a grateful smile, thinking of all the times she'd snuck the twins snacks in similar situations.

I did enjoy the preaching. It was refreshing to hear a man with such passion. The rise and fall of his voice reminded me of the Baptist hell-fire-and-brimstone preachers of my youth more than the carefully crafted lectures at my current church. His message, however, centered on praise for God and love for neighbors instead of eternal flames. I also enjoyed the give-and-take between the pastor and the congregation with their shouts of "Amen, brother!" and "That's right!" punctuating each point. It seemed more communal than the staid lessons I was accustomed to.

I had feared mine would be the only white face in the crowd, but there were a few mixed-race couples sprinkled throughout. What struck me most, though, was that the people weren't that much different from me and the people I knew. Mothers were trying to keep their kids from peeking over pews and hamming it up for the people behind them. A grandmother opened her purse for peppermints and passed them down the row to a person struggling with a cough. Teenage boys stole glances at a group of girls on the opposite side. I also liked how nobody who shook my hand at the beginning asked me what I "did" for a living or what brought me here today. They simply welcomed me into their space.

So, now I've written all of this, and I've hardly mentioned Ruthie. That's because I barely noticed she was there. I was so caught up in the service that I didn't have time to think about her and all our troubles. After the service, Josh and I left together, following many good-byes and expressing our appreciation for the invitation.

Josh reached over and took my hand as we walked in silence toward home. I didn't say anything for fear of disturbing the rare amicable moment. When we reached the front porch, he stopped, leaned down and kissed me gently on the cheek. "Thank you, beautiful girl, for going today. I know it wasn't easy for you."

I doubt he had any idea how difficult it had been for me to walk in those doors, but looking back at those terrifying moments before I did, I wonder exactly what I'd been afraid of.

Dear Corel,

I haven't been this happy since Abby knocked on Ruthie's front door! Well done, faithful warrior. We see and celebrate your patience and tireless efforts. Look at the wonderful fruit of all those nights you spent standing watch outside Abby's bedroom guarding against the fiery darts of our enemies, quenching their missiles of anger, outrage, and self-righteousness with the healing balm of wisdom, beauty, and humility.

Speaking of humility, I love yours—acknowledging how the prayers for Abby make you stronger, enabling you to interrupt the demons' attacks and break through their strongholds. Yes, it is a group effort, but you play the main role. Abby thinks she was alone. She has no idea all the prayers that buoyed her at every moment, or the demons who tried to prevent her, as she walked down the sidewalk into that church.

Can you imagine how events like the girls' night out and going to church with Ruthie might have played out a few months ago without all your efforts? The battle is far from over, of course, and we must continue to be vigilant, but today is a day of celebration! Abby's soul is squarely on the path to redemption. Drink your fill of the joy that comes from turning Our Lord's beloved back toward Him!

For His Glory,

Ariam

Stumbletrick:

I've alerted the authorities. I can't see any way around this for you. Of course, we're not removing you from the case just yet. Like a wound caused by a projectile, one can often do more damage by a reckless wrenching of the offending object, so we're leaving you in place for now.

However, we have to move into triage mode due to your catastrophic failure. Try to compose yourself. Hysterics will do you no good. I saw this coming from the beginning and prepared for this eventuality. Shameglut will now be consulting as well. That's how bad it is.

You've blown our cover to smithereens. She is beginning to recognize her sins of selfishness and pride, so now we've got two choices: get her to defend herself or get her to turn away from these relationships all together. It's not too late for either. Personally, I'd love to see her justify her sin. Even a demon with your lack of vision can understand the possibilities of embracing and defending unabashed white supremacy. I don't see her going down that road, though.

If we can no longer downplay the damage done by her haughtiness, enter Shameglut. He will beat the victim over the head with shame for her self-righteousness and superior attitude. I would suggest using her friends, but Shameglut's been an expert for millennia, so let's make use of him. I'm sure he can enlighten you on the best methods, so you can at least assist in his efforts. Nothing she can do will ever make up for her sin, but we can sure have fun convincing her to try.

See if you can follow the delicious irony: she feels guilty for her haughtiness to others, so to ease her guilt and do penance she berates others for thinking themselves superior. Then, in her mind she *proves* herself superior yet again and starts the cycle all over. Classic log-in-your-own-eye stuff.

That's what I would do, but again, ask Shameglut. I'm washing my hands of this mess. I'm not going to the torturers with any of you over this.

Needless to say, I hope we never work together again after this assignment. For that matter, I'm not sure you will ever escape punishment. But on the off-chance you do, you could do worse than to take note of how when one deception has been foiled, a master like me pivots and starts right in on the next one.

Always your superior—

Twisttale

ABBY'S JOURNAL

Wednesday, March 24th —

Josh claims it will be okay if we give up—not try to legally protect or defend ourselves, admit our fault, and throw ourselves at her mercy.

He's so naive. That's not how the real world works. He says everything will be okay. He doesn't know that. He can't know that. He only says that because he doesn't care about the same things I do. He doesn't care about losing the house, or about our kids' inheritance, or about how we will look to our friends and business associates, or even just folks who read the paper if we admit to having mistreated our employee. Who will want me to sell their house then? Who will want us on their party invite list or even on their Christmas card list? But he doesn't think about things like that. He's never cared about those things.

Losing our home, reputation, and future wouldn't be okay. It would be horrible.

Admitting guilt in private is one thing, but when you put things in legal documents, those consequences last forever. Next thing you know, Ruthie will be living in our house, and we'll be making payments to her in perpetuity. Stranger things have happened. When McDonald's sold that woman a $2 cup of hot coffee, they didn't think that they would end up paying her millions. Courts do crazy things.

Power also does crazy things. Ruthie seems like a reasonable, decent person most of the time, but give a person the opportunity to hurt you without consequence and few can resist. No, I can't risk it. *We* can't risk it.

But Josh won't go along with me on this one. Am I willing to throw away our marriage over a lawsuit? Damn you, Ruthie! Why are you doing this to us?

Thursday, March 25th —

I probably shouldn't put these thoughts on paper, but I can't help wishing Ruthie would disappear. Everything was fine before. Why did she have to stir everything up? I wish we'd never met her. I wish I hadn't asked her to come work for us.

But that's not true. Our family wouldn't have been the same without her. I honestly don't think we could have survived without her, though I had forgotten it in recent years. When we first moved in, she saw me struggling with two babies, and she offered to hold Destiny while I changed Cash. I was so grateful. At the time, I felt like I was drowning. I invited her in for coffee, and in her Ruthie-way, she made everything better just by being there. She poured her own coffee. She entertained Cash with a funny song while she bounced Destiny on her knee, allowing me to run to the bathroom alone during the day for the first time in forever. Within thirty minutes, I was pulling out my purse and begging her not to go.

So no, I don't wish I'd never met her. I thanked God for her for years and years. In hindsight, maybe I should have said thanks a little less to God and a little more to her. Then again, somewhere along the line, I forgot to say thanks to anyone. Like I did with Josh, I took her and her gifts for granted. When I didn't need her as much, her habits, like all those little games and traditions she and the kids had together, seemed annoying, not helpful. The inevitable inconveniences of having another person in my life and in my house started to grate.

I could have been kinder, more generous. I could have included her in more things. I could have stood up for her when others were downright mean, like that birthday party when Destiny's friend's mother told Ruthie the time to be back for pickup when she could see other adults staying for the festivities. But I didn't. And for that, I'm sorry. But I still don't think that justifies her suing us. And I don't think I need to hand over the keys to our house, which Josh is essentially suggesting we do.

I'll ask the girls at brunch what they think.

Saturday, March 27th —

Boy, did I get an earful! I thought they would take my side about the lawsuit, but they spent most of their time talking about me going to Ruthie's church. You'd think a white person going to a Black church is some kind of crime. The most passionate tirade came from Ivy, of course. No one dares to say anything to contradict her because a) it's just not worth it, b) it will only make her tirades worse, and c) it will trigger her Rejection Sensitive Dysphoria (i.e. – she can't handle being criticized), which she claims to have gotten from her upbringing by strict mid-western parents who believed in spanking. But for someone who can't tolerate criticism, she sure does heap a lot of it on everyone else.

I don't even want to go into it. I didn't even understand some of it. She threw out phrases like *sacred spaces, unintentionally perpetuating harm, cultural appropriation, enslaver/settler theology,* and a few things about *colonial bias.*

Why am I still friends with her?

As if that wasn't bad enough, Jessica called when I got home. "The girls and I were talking after you left."

Of course, they were.

"Don't you think it's really weird that Josh called Ruthie and was talking to her about you?"

Shocking. Unlike the fact that my friends were talking about me— unashamedly, apparently—after I left.

But Jessica couldn't hear my snarky thoughts. "Do you think there's something there?"

"What do you mean?"

"I mean, why would he do that?"

They didn't even know about Ruthie's other comment—that I should ask Josh why she thought this battle with me was worth fighting. I was so frightened of opening that Pandora's box, I hardly admitted it to myself.

"I don't know what you're insinuating, Jessica," I responded coldly, although I knew *exactly* what she was insinuating. "I'm sure he just thought he could help smooth things over."

"Any man of mine talking to another woman about me behind my back would be hearing about it, and so would she."

"Well, I'm not you." I was proud of myself for my dispassionate tone. "Josh and I trust each other. Thanks for your concern, but that's the least of my worries."

For all my bravado on the phone, I was a mess. What was going on between Josh and Ruthie? I didn't think it was anything romantic, but what had Ruthie meant with that cryptic comment about me asking Josh why she chose to pick this fight? I couldn't keep from replaying Ivy's criticisms in my head and mulling over Jessica's lurid suggestion.

I needed someone to help me sort it all out. So, I called Shirley.

"No matter what I do, I can't please anyone," I cried to my friend, my eyes filling with angry, defeated tears. "I am shamed no matter what: if I go to church, if I stay away, if I speak up, if I keep silent, if I ask questions, if I don't."

"I'm sorry, girlie," Shirley said. "But it sounds like you need to talk to Josh."

Oh brother, not that again. "I can't talk to him!" I wailed. "I'm afraid of what he'll say. I don't think I can handle the truth. Whatever it is, it can't be good. I'd almost rather live in ignorance just a little while longer."

"You know what the Good Book says about knowing the truth—it will set you free."

"I've never really understood that verse."

"You don't have to understand. Just believe. It's called faith."

Stumbletrick,

See, you fool? She's right back in her old patterns—navel-gazing, doubting her husband, blaming Ruthie, defending herself, listening to her friends, confused and isolated. I told you those roots run deep. Just watch. I'm going to snap that marriage in two, just like you should have done ages ago.

Our organization has suffered some significant punctures in our defenses as a direct result of your unbelievable incompetence, but I've built such a truly impressive infrastructure here on the North American continent that even after blow upon blow, the foundation still stands. Once I finish off this target, I'm sure the powers below will take note and finally recognize my brilliance, as well as your incompetence.

In the meantime, keep lobbing relentless attacks. She'll succumb. And when she does, I'll make sure it hurts so badly that she never dares to veer again. That's the great thing about the straight and narrow path. Not only is it really hard to walk down, it's really easy to fall off.

Watch and learn —

Twisttale

ABBY'S JOURNAL

Sunday, March 28ᵗʰ —

I don't know why I let myself get my hopes up about Josh. I should have known better than to think that a few laughs or moments of connection meant we could find common ground. He's made it clear where he stands on the lawsuit, and it's not with me. But it's not just the lawsuit. It's everything. He does his thing, and I do mine. We don't communicate. It's so different from how it used to be.

I remember when we were newlyweds. Or even further back, when we were dating, when I felt like he saw me. Nothing thrilled me more than that deep intense gaze of his. It melted me into butter. One look, one kiss—his touch was electric—it was all I could think about for days. I wanted nothing more than to be with him—to hear him laugh, even watch him work.

I had been so jaded back then, suffered so many false starts, so many disappointments. I wondered if I was past feeling that exhilarating infatuation anymore. I still remember our first date, when he gallantly draped his coat, still warm and smelling of him, over my shoulders and put his hand gently on my back to guide me confidently through the crowd on the London Underground. I know it sounds silly, but every other guy I'd ever dated faded right out of my mind at that moment. Where has this guy been? I knew right away that he was the one I had been waiting for.

Even my sorrows couldn't last long when I was with him. He'd wrap me in his arms as I poured out my heart. He'd stroke my back like I was a child and whisper in my ear that it would be all right. And it always was. As long as Josh loved me, all the world around us could spin off course but I would be safe and warm and held.

What happened? How did we drift so far apart?

Monday, March 29th —

Well, I did it. I talked to Josh.

After dinner, I came up behind him, gathered my courage, and asked point blank why he had called Ruthie. I asked why he was talking to her about me and why she suggested he would know the answer about why she chose to fight this battle with us. And just like I predicted, it was a disaster.

He wouldn't give me a straight answer. I'm so tired of his cryptic statements. What can I do but assume the worst? I'd intended to be calm and unemotional, to listen to him and echo back what he said—all the things I know I'm supposed to do during a conflict. But once I opened the door, I couldn't stem the flood. All the insecurities and resentment I'd been gathering up for months—no, years—spilled out.

When I finished my rant, the empty house sounded eerily silent. He stood from the sofa where I had ambushed him and walked toward me, his voice quiet. "I never shamed you, Abby."

"Well, it feels like it." I raged. "You let others shame me. You let Ruthie sue me. You talk to her about me behind my back, and instead of sticking up for me, you took her side and made me feel like it was my fault."

I was hysterical now. My pitch was high, my words coming too fast, breaking over my sobs. "Why? Why would you encourage Ruthie to *sue* us? Why would you choose her over me? Over your own family?" I wanted to break things, to slap him. But I ended up crumpled in a heap on the floor sobbing, beating my fists against the floor.

He put his hand on my back, but I screamed, "Don't touch me!"

He kneeled in front of me and took my wrists and held them in his grasp.

"Leave me alone!" I tried to yank them back, but he didn't let go. He held firm and stayed calm.

"I won't." His tone was gentle, calm, and kind. "I won't leave you alone. I won't let you hurt yourself like this. I won't let you tell yourself these lies."

"So only you are allowed to hurt me? It's *loving* to your wife to take away our home? To expose all her faults? To betray her?"

Never in a million years would I have expected betrayal from him.

Distant? Sometimes. Cold? It could feel like it. Judgmental? Sure seemed that way to me, especially recently. But back-stabbing? I couldn't believe it, and the pain was like a knife in my chest.

"I love you, Abby." Josh's quiet words disrupted my internal tirade and pulled it out into the open. I jerked away from his grasp, struggled to my feet, and stood looking down at him.

"Then why don't you support me? Why don't you say anything nice? You leave everything up to me. You send me out with Ruthie alone. I ask you what you think, and you give these impossible answers. Then I do my best, and you waltz in all disapproving after I've invested tons of time and energy."

He doesn't love me the way a husband should. He loves me in a pitying, pious, saint-saving-a-sinner sort of way. Who wants that? I can't live under the weight of that judgment.

He stood now as well, taking in my verbal assault, his eyes so sad. And tired. "Abby, life is not always the way it seems to you." He held out his arms. "I love you, even if you don't see it. Trust me. I am in this with you. I want us to be together."

I almost caved. I almost melted and gave up, but then I remembered all the hurt that he could have stopped and didn't. He didn't just let it happen. He encouraged it. I wanted to believe we'd turned a corner, but there's no solution. I turned and walked away. I'm trying to open up my heart, but he doesn't seem willing to change, or compromise, or see things from my perspective. Maybe I'm the one with Rejection Sensitive Dysphoria. But regardless, I can't handle this pain.

Dearest Corel,

You're right. She holds on so tightly to her chains. It breaks my heart, too. She's afraid of the very thing that will set her free.

Oh, why won't she repent, confess, and turn to Our Lord! Her sins would be washed away. She would become purer than the whitest snow. Forgiveness, cleansing, and healing are there, waiting for her. Don't give up, Corel!

All the beauty. All the freedom. I wish we could simply yell, "Give up, Abby! Let go! Let Our Lord love and guide you. Joy awaits!" But we can't rip open the chrysalis, remember? She has to come to that realization for herself.

Sometimes the hardest part is holding back and waiting.

Hold strong, warrior,

Ariam

CHAPTER TWENTY

Porch Confessions

ABBY'S JOURNAL

Spy Wednesday, March 31st —

Josh had given me no answers, so I asked Ruthie.

I invited her over for a glass of lemonade on the porch. We had been enjoying the breeze and listening to the gentle rise and fall of the occasional passing cars' engines before I broached the dreaded subject.

"Why now, Ruthie? Why, after all these years did you decide to sue us? I know I haven't always treated you the way I should, but I thought we were on the same team. I thought you cared about us. Why didn't you just talk to me? Why go straight to a lawsuit instead of a conversation?"

"I don't owe you an explanation." Her expression gave nothing away.

Obviously, Ruthie wasn't going to make this easy. I know she didn't have to. But I needed to understand, so I tried again. "If you'd like to tell me, I promise to listen."

"Don't make promises you can't keep."

I let slip a smile, remembering how well Ruthie knew me.

She let her face break into a grin as well.

"All I can do is my best," I promised. "It's not that great, as you well know, but I can try. How about if I guess, and you say yes or no?"

"Oh, good grief! That's the worst idea you've come up with yet. Just sit still for a minute, and I'll try to tell you, since you're going to start making up your own crazy ideas if I don't."

We rocked in silence until I wondered if she was going to tell me today or if I was going to have to wait even longer.

"It was Jessica," Ruthie finally said.

"Jessica? What on earth does she have to do with us?"

"I thought you said you were going to listen."

"Sorry." Chastened, I pressed my lips together and nodded.

"Abby, I know you as well as anyone. I've been in your house, cared for your kids, and watched everything you do for almost two decades. I know you think you're better than me. You have always thought yourself superior."

Considering I'd already admitted as much, I saw no point in responding. I gave her a go-ahead nod.

"It's not okay. It's wrong, but it is what it is. Your problem, not mine. I've got my own problems. But because of your superiority complex, you don't put up a front for me. Half the time, you barely realize I'm around. You never cared what you let me see."

Where was she going with all this? What on earth could she have seen that would make her turn on us? I can't think of any skeletons hidden in the closet.

"I saw you agonize over helping Jessica," Ruthie said finally. "I saw you weep."

Yes, I did. My heart was broken for my friend and the child in her womb, and I was distressed about how to help. I still don't know what Jessica decided after talking to Josh that night. She hasn't told me, and I haven't asked. I think it might be better that way.

Ruthie stopped rocking and stared at the street as she spoke. "You never wept for my baby. You gave me time off work—even a sabbatical when the kids went to school. You gave me extra money and a ride even if I didn't say what I needed it for. But you didn't stay with me, and you didn't cry."

I stopped rocking as well. It was the only time we'd ever spoken of Ruthie's pregnancy since she confided in me so many years ago. I try hard never to think of it, to move on, to forget the past, to do better. I pressed my lips together, trying to keep my promise.

"For the next thirteen years, I liked to think you cared about me—not as much as you cared about yourself, of course." She managed a weak smile.

I tried to return it, but I couldn't.

"But I believed that you were trying your best ... until I saw you torn up about Jessica. Then I couldn't pretend anymore."

She turned and met my eyes, "I answered your question, so let me ask you mine: Why didn't you cry over my baby's life like you did hers?"

My head and my heart were pounding. That fight-or-flight instinct is real. But I chose the third less-talked-about alternative. I froze. What could I say?

Nothing.

For once in my life, I was glad to keep my mouth shut.

Because every word was true. I cared about Jessica and her baby more than Ruthie and hers. I didn't want to deny it, but I couldn't admit it either. What kind of person would that make me?

When Ruthie needed help all those years ago, I didn't show her the same concern I'd shown Jessica. I may have asked the same question—"What do you want to do?"—but we both knew the words hadn't carried the same meaning in my heart.

Ruthie had exposed my greatest shame. We might not have spoken the words, even to one another, but her baby's blood was on my hands as much, if not more, than it was on hers. I'd never admitted my part to anyone—not my girlfriends, not my life coach, not even my journal—and especially not Josh. Why did I see Ruthie's pregnancy differently from Jessica's? Perhaps because her pregnancy was inconvenient *for me*. It would have disrupted my life. It would have been expensive to hire another qualified helper. I let economics and my own agenda overshadow the heartbreak of this person close to me and the life of a small child.

And, of course, I couldn't deny that her race influenced my reaction. Was I really one of the racist bigots people talk about? How could that be? If that was true, how could I forgive myself? And if I couldn't forgive myself, how could I expect anyone else to forgive me?

Shame washed over me, ugly and sticky like the thickest pitch. Not just from that event but from all of it. Sins I'd committed years before joined those from that very morning, flashing across the screen of my mind like a slideshow.

My way of coping with shame had always been to bury it deep and forget it, but there, in the dark corners of my heart, it grew. Strangely, those roots of resentment had wrapped tightly not only around my heart but Ruthie's as well, and fear of exposure had sprouted in the middle of my marriage, pushing Josh and me further and further apart.

In a feeble attempt to escape the excruciating pain of her gaze, her judgment, I closed my eyes. The muscle memory triggered that old familiar instinct, and I found myself praying.

One word: *Help.*

I lifted my head, opened my eyes, and turned haltingly to Ruthie. She was still looking at me, but she wasn't smirking in derision. She wasn't triumphant. She wasn't even angry. Her dark brown eyes were unspeakably sad. Her brown cheeks were wet with tears. I no longer saw an enemy who wanted to hurt me and my family. I saw a wounded friend.

Before I was even fully aware of what I was doing, I slid out of my chair and down to my knees in front of her. "I am so sorry," I choked out. "I was wrong. I didn't help you like I could have, and even worse I didn't care as much as I should have. I can't undo that. You are right, and I was wrong. I am so sorry."

Ruthie's muscle memory must have kicked in, too, because she placed her hand on my lowered head and smoothed my hair like I'd seen her do with my kids hundreds of times.

When I felt the weight of her hand resting on my scalp, I realized she had never touched me before. I know I'd never touched her.

I didn't deserve to be comforted. I didn't deserve her forgiveness. I dropped lower, my forehead on the concrete, outside of her reach, as sobs rippled through me.

"Get up, Abby." She patted my back with a maternal air. "I appreciate you getting down there, but it's not a place either of us wants you to stay."

Wiping the tears from my eyes, I struggled back into the chair. We both rocked, sniffed, and wiped away our tears.

"I wanted to hurt you." Ruthie's confession broke the silence. "That's why I did it. I wanted to hurt you like you hurt me."

Wow. So now we're both being honest.

"I don't care about the money. I wanted others to know how you disregarded me and my feelings all those years, how you looked right through me, how you ran over me and treated me like dirt. I wanted you to know that, too, and be exposed and feel ashamed."

Ruthie let out a long, slow breath. "I guess I'm saying I'm sorry, too, Abby."

We sat for a long time, neither saying a word, only the soft cooing of a dove adding melody to the quiet between us. The temperature of the air felt like it dropped ten degrees. My face no longer burned with shame. When I gained my composure, I wiped my cheeks a final time. "Where do we go from here?"

"I don't know. I can imagine you going back into your big beautiful house and your busy life and thinking you've solved the problem by being just a little less inconsiderate."

"I can imagine that, too," I quietly admitted. Funny how things seemed clearer now. "How do we prevent that?" I held my breath, waiting, hoping she'd have an answer.

"Just because I know the problem doesn't mean I know the solution!" The joy from her wide grin washed over both of us.

I really, really wanted to suggest a mediator for the lawsuit, but instead, I said, "How about we start with praying together?"

"That's one of the smartest things I've ever heard you say, Abby. I'll start."

Oh, Corel, the joy in Heaven!

Your heavenly audience is glorifying Our Lord and praising you, oh mighty and clever warrior, for this critical breakthrough! This is what we've been praying for—for Abby to admit her sins and bring them out into the open so they can be cleansed and healed. Oh, that beautiful prayer, that one word cry for help in faith and trust, echoed throughout the universe and stirred all of Heaven to her side.

And then for Ruthie to admit hers as well! That was even more than I had hoped. They are untouchable by our enemies when joined together in prayer. Hallelujah!

I love how you wasted no time in landing a powerful blow on that sneaky demon the very moment Abby prayed. You sliced right through that veil that had been blinding both of them from seeing each other as God sees them—as beautiful daughters of Our Lord Himself. Oh, it was so beautiful to see them beholding one another as the immortal souls they are, starting on a mutual path toward redemption and love.

But your tour de force wasn't a tactical combat maneuver. You've grown so much. You helped Abby to her knees—that moment we all longed for when she fell to the ground in repentance. And then kneeling beside her, you gave her the strength to utter the hardest words for humans to say, "I was wrong."

Glory Hallelujah! A great victory was won today. But get back in there, soldier! We know our enemy will be doubling their forces now.

Victory is near! You can do it!

Ariam

No time to lick your wounds, Stumbletrick!

I don't care what he did to you. Any demon so incompetent as to let their victim call out directly for divine help deserves what they get from a Guardian. That's the point of this whole operation! We are deceivers!

We are now outgunned, you numbskull. Every single human potentially has an army of angels at their beck and call. They are just too shortsighted, thinking that since they can't see them with their physical eyes, they must not be there. You know why they think that? Because most of us are doing our job!

Back to work! Time is short. Neutralizing the conflict with Ruthie is a huge blow, but don't let all that long-held anger and resentment go to waste. Find somewhere else to channel it. Like at her husband. Don't let him off the hook. Destroying the marriage is still the key.

No excuses! Do something! Get in there and fight like your life depends on it.

Because believe me, it does—

Twisttale

CHAPTER TWENTY-ONE
Surprised by Grace

ABBY'S JOURNAL

Maundy Thursday, April 1st —

"Sit with me, Abby." Josh took my hand and tried to lead me to the sofa.

"I can't," I said. "I have too much to do."

Inside, I fumed. I know he's trying to be sweet. But all I can think is, are you kidding me? Do you even know me? Things might be a little more friendly between Ruthie and me now. And yes, Josh deserves some credit for that. But I'm still mad at him. He doesn't get to make me feel bad about myself, expect me to do everything, and then instruct me to come and sit beside him when I have so much to do.

"Let me help you," he said.

I know this is what I've been wanting, but instead of being grateful, I find myself resenting that he didn't offer earlier. He's usually too busy with his work and the things he cares about to help with my things.

I lifted a giant accordion file folder from under the desk. "We need to document everything we paid Ruthie over the years, all written contracts we've had, all the emails or texts we've exchanged regarding overtime, insurance documents, receipts, check stubs—"

"You don't need to gather those things anymore." He took the folder from my hands and put it back under the desk.

"The attorney said he needed them as soon as possible," I argued.

"I'm going to work it out."

"Without me?"

"That's what I wanted to talk to you about tonight. I want to do this with you."

"But we can't pay what she's asking."

"*We* can't, but I can. We'll have to sell the house."

I felt the blood rush from my face. Sell the house? Sell our *house*? Just like that?

"And I've asked my dad for a portion of my inheritance."

Not only was he giving away our kids' inheritance, but he was giving away his own? That was bad enough, but the way he talked about it, like it was nothing.

"Abby, I know you don't agree or understand why we need to do this, but we do. Please trust me. You don't have to worry. I will always take care of you."

I couldn't breathe. I couldn't see straight. Talk about a gut punch. I fumbled to find a chair away from Josh and to process what he was saying.

The rest of the night is a blur—confusion, screaming, crying, pleading. The man is insane. He wants to give away our house *and* his inheritance and expects me to do nothing? It's one thing for the court to take it from us, but for him to give it up voluntarily? It's beyond the pale.

If I needed definitive proof that Josh didn't care about me, I sure have it now.

Good Friday, April 2nd —

Josh plans to sell the house and give away part of his inheritance to Ruthie to settle the lawsuit.

I'm still stunned.

I don't even know what to say. This isn't how I thought our marriage would end. It's not about the money. We started with nothing. His inheritance was never mine in the first place. I guess he can give it to whomever he wants. It's the betrayal. It's that he would *want* to it to go to someone else, not to us or to our children. It's that he wouldn't fight to protect us. To protect me.

`Holy Saturday, April 3ʳᵈ —`

It's over. I can't stay.

I can't live with a man who would turn his back on his wife and children. It's too hard. There's nothing left for me here in this graveyard of promises. Our marriage is dead—nothing left but the empty shell of appearance. I haven't told him. I'm not even sure I'll pack my things. I don't have the energy. I think I'll leave it all behind and start over.

Not until Monday though, because tomorrow we have the big Easter get-together with his family. It's a huge deal—all the extended family plus more guests than I can keep track of will be at his father's estate. If I leave today, I'll be the topic of every conversation tomorrow. I've got to keep going through the motions one day more.

Dear Stumbletrick,

One day more, and I will no longer have to deal with your incompetence and imbecilic comments. Looks like we finally destroyed the marriage against all odds. Maybe you just needed a little pressure. You've finally managed, with significant heavy lifting from yours truly and a little from Shameglut, to accomplish in four months what could have been knocked out in a few weeks.

I'll assemble the troops for the final blow. I doubt your services will be required any longer on this continent. Thanks to you, it is highly unlikely that the services of any other Eastern demons will be sought any time soon either.

Hasta la vista, moron—

Twisttale

Dear Corel,

Keep faith, my friend.

Abby may not see a way forward, but we know Our Lord will make one. He will never leave her or stop fighting for her ... and neither will we.

Our demonic foes may believe they have her in their grasp, but the fervent prayers of the righteous give us strength. The time of the final battle draws nigh. Our Lord will deliver our enemies into our hands. Let us be ready to come to His side as He fights for His beloved!

For the Glory of God,

Ariam

ABBY'S JOURNAL

Easter Sunday, April 4th —

"Abby." My father-in-law called to me as I walked by the mahogany-paneled doorway to his private inner sanctum. I had arrived at Easter brunch by myself a bit late, desperately wanting to be invisible and get through the event without crying or causing a scene.

I froze at the sound of his voice. I'd never been in his study before. Come to think of it, I'd never been alone with him. To be honest, I've always been a little afraid of him. Despite his kindness, his voice drips with authority, and I have heard stories of his anger. Had he guessed I was planning to leave? Maybe if I turned away fast enough, I could pretend I didn't hear.

"I want to talk with you," he called again.

Scared but unwilling to disobey, I stepped inside and moved toward the tufted leather chair where he was sitting in front of an enormous stone fireplace. Instead of standing or pulling up a seat, though, I sank to my knees on the Persian rug at his feet.

"Yes, Dad?"

"Abby, you are my daughter. You are part of our family, and I love you." His well-intended words rang empty in my ears. If he only knew all the things I'd done, he'd be the first in line to kick me out of his beloved family.

As if reading my mind, he shook his head, offering me a sad smile. "I want you to know that nothing you do will ever change that love—not anything. I can forgive you for anything—except leaving my son."

I hadn't told anyone my plan to leave Josh, but he must have guessed I wouldn't exactly love Josh's plan to sell the house and give up his inheritance. He probably just doesn't want the shame of divorce in the family.

"I know all about the struggles you've had."

My eyes dropped to the floor as heat rose in my cheeks. How could he know? I stole a glance at his face. The sorrow and seriousness revealed in the reflected light from the fire removed any doubt. He knew. My head bowed in shame, and my eyes rested on his wrinkled hands. He held one out to me.

"I wish you had come to me and asked for help." No longer the authoritarian, his voice held the same kindness as Josh's when he spoke with the kids. "You know I would have been happy to help you—and your friends, too, if you had asked."

I grasped his offered hand in both of mine and tried to stop the tears from falling to no avail. I didn't deserve this. I didn't deserve his love. Regret and fear filled my heart, but they mingled with something new—hope for forgiveness and the unconditional love I'd longed for.

"Abby, don't leave us." This time his voice held a plea instead of a command.

"I don't want to," I managed to choke out.

This dear man knew my guilt and still wanted me in his family. His acceptance sunk in like warm oil on the parched skin of my too-much rejected heart. Still clinging to his hand but too ashamed to look into his eyes, I stared into the fire as I leaned against his knee.

I wanted to believe—in love, in forgiveness, in mercy—but hurt and fear gripped my heart, pulling me back.

"I'm so sorry, but I don't think I can stay. I don't want to drag you into all of this, but Josh doesn't love me anymore. He doesn't want me. He stays with me because he's so good, because he took a vow. But I feel his condemnation and judgment all the time, and I can't bear it."

Tears streamed down my cheeks. With his free hand, Dad lifted my face and gently wiped away the tears. "Of course, he loves you. But I see you won't believe my words, so I will show you."

He lifted a carved wooden box from the side table. "Joshua sees you as I do, as you were created to be. He knows what you've done, but he chooses to see who you really are and loves you no matter what." He handed the box to me.

It weighed much more than I would have expected, considering its size. I placed it on my lap and ran my hands across the smooth walnut lid inlaid with two crossing bands of cherry.

"Take it to him and let him show you."

I couldn't imagine what could be in that box that would change my mind, but what else could I do? It felt impossible to disobey his command, nor did I want to. I struggled to my feet. Despite the heavy burden in my hands, I pushed my way through the crowded rooms. The closer I got to where I thought Josh must be, the more desperate I felt. Almost running, I burst into the packed great room, searching in the chaos for my husband, not caring that I probably looked like a mascara-smeared crazy woman.

I found him sitting among the children of the extended family and guests.

Without preliminaries, I stepped in front of him. It took all my strength to present the box at arm's length. All the chatter in the room ceased, and everyone stared. Despite having their game interrupted, the children seemed as curious as I was to see inside the mysterious container. Josh stood and lifted its weight from my hands.

"Truce?" He smiled, and I saw the familiar glint of love and joy in his eyes.

"Your dad gave it to me. He said it would prove you love me."

"Did he now?" he said in a playful tone loud enough for all to hear. Still calm, still perfect, Josh responded as if one of the children had given him a dandelion instead of his screwed-up wife making a scene asking him to prove his love in the middle of a party.

He put his hand on my back and ushered me through the crowd to a drawing room I'd never seen before where we could be alone. I welcomed the privacy from all the prying eyes as I silently wondered how many rooms were in this massive house.

Alone, he led me to a velvet loveseat and sat beside me, setting the box on a low coffee table in front of us. Completely serious now, he looked me straight in the eyes and asked, "Where were you earlier today, Abby?"

I was so tired of hiding from him, of masking my true feelings and actions for fear of his judgment. We were at the end. There no longer seemed any reason to hold back.

"Packing—I'm leaving. For good. I don't see this marriage lasting. I don't believe you truly love me. Frankly, I don't think you even like me anymore. We're too different. Your father caught me as I was sneaking in late, trying to avoid a scene. He told me to bring this box to you and that it might change my mind, but I can't imagine that it will."

His deep brown eyes never left mine. "What do you want, Abby?"

"I want the same thing every woman, every person wants—to be seen and loved, to be safe and secure, to be soothed and told it's all going to be all right." My voice broke. "What I don't want and what I can't stand any longer is to be shamed and judged."

"Do you love me?"

His question surprised me enough that I didn't answer immediately. Before I could push the response, *Of course I love you,* past the lump in my throat, Josh continued.

"I love *you* this much." He pried the two sections of the box apart. A small avalanche of paper spilled out on the table. Photos, receipts, cards, invitations, and more.

Confused, I sorted through the haphazard collage. I spotted a dinner receipt from at least twenty years before. The printed numbers had faded with age but Josh's hand-written five-hundred-dollar tip and "Blessings to you, Philip" scrawled at the bottom still stood out clearly.

I remember that restaurant. It was the only time we ever went because the service was awful. I'm sure Philip wasn't the waiter's real name; he barely understood English and was so rude to me that I reported him to his manager. Back then, I would have been furious if I had known Josh had added that whopping tip, but I can see now that I over-reacted to the situation.

Next, an elegant card caught my eye. A laser-cut bouquet of blossoms popped up as I opened it and read, "Thank you, Josh, for the amazing dinner at Chez Grâce! So sorry Abby couldn't make it, but we had such a lovely time. Next time drinks at our place – Ted and Mike." Josh had taken our gay neighbors to the fanciest restaurant in town without inviting me? Why? I mean, I wouldn't have gone anyway. He knows how I feel about their lifestyle. But what's with all these secrets?

So far, he wasn't off to a great start on proving he loves me. "I don't understand," I mumbled as I continued to sift through the pile.

I picked up a tri-fold brochure with "Welcome to The Sanctuary" in an elaborate sage green scroll across the front and a yellow hand-written Post-It note stuck to it that read "*Jessica.*"

"What is this?" I asked. "And why does it have Jessica's name on it?" As usual, Josh wasn't quick to answer. I kept it in my hand as I scanned the other photos on the table of joyful children, gathered families, and celebrations. I didn't recognize any of them.

And then I did.

I gasped as I saw a photo of Ruthie holding a baby—a beautiful little girl with dark curls and deep dimples. I dropped the brochure, and with shaking hands, I opened the packet clipped to the photo. As I pulled out a birth certificate, adoption papers, report cards, hand-drawn pictures, and letters, the truth began to dawn on me. Ruthie had her baby after all. She hadn't gone through with the abortion.

And Josh had known the whole time—about her pregnancy, me taking her to the clinic, about the fact that I'd try to hide it—all of it. That's why he insisted on us giving her a nine-month sabbatical fourteen years ago, not because the twins went to school full-time. They had shared this secret all these years.

Josh moved closer and put his arm around me. He whispered even though we were the only people in the room. "The choices you made weren't right, Abby." More judgment and condemnation? I couldn't bear to look him in the face. I no longer wanted to argue and defend myself. I straightened my back, pressed my lips together, and steeled myself to hear what he had to say no matter how difficult it might be.

Instead of the expected sigh of disappointment, though, I heard a smile in his voice as he said, "We fixed it—Dad and I. All of it. There is no guilt, and there is no shame. Ruthie called me from the clinic that day and told me everything. We came and got her and arranged the help she needed. You can look at these precious faces and know that it's all been covered and redeemed."

I stared at the pile of images. The enormity of what he was saying was only starting to sink in.

"Every item in this box represents a beautiful story, priceless souls cared for and uplifted. What did Joseph tell his brothers? They intended harm, but God intended it for good, to accomplish the saving of many lives. This box is a testament to the saving of many lives. Ruthie's little girl was only one of them."

I turned toward him now. "I don't understand. You went behind me and cleaned up all my messes and mistakes? Why? And how could you still love me if you knew everything I've done?"

He took my face in his hands and gently wiped away my tears. "I love you. I want to be with you. You are my wife, and I cherish you. I didn't want anything to come between us. And it doesn't have to."

All the times I hadn't been able to admit I was wrong, probably because I knew it was too much to ever make right, Josh had faced those wrongs for me—he and his father together. He hadn't ratted me out. Instead, he forgave me each moment and covered my guilt. They had done the work, paid the price, immersed themselves in all the ugliness I caused, and transformed those messes into the happy endings laid out in front of me now. This was evidence even I couldn't deny. Josh did love me. He still loves me. Only passionate, all-consuming, nobody-but-you love does something like this.

"Do you love me, Abby?" he asked for a second time.

I looked down again and mumbled, "I want to, but I don't understand you. How could you love me when you know about all my ugliness? And

I still don't know why you are selling our house after everything you have already done for Ruthie. Or why you take Ruthie's side over mine every time. Or why you didn't you even tell me about all these things."

He gently tilted my face up toward his and brushed back my hair. "Why didn't *you* tell *me* about them?" The question pierced my heart. It was true. I hadn't wanted his help or advice because I had known what he would say.

Josh continued, "I would have loved to have shared all these moments with you. Don't you know I wanted to work together to redeem and restore each of these situations? But you didn't trust me with them. You tried to hide them and keep me at arm's length." He leaned his forehead against mine.

"Love trusts, Abby. I need you to trust me. And love sacrifices. Can you drink from this cup?"

Oh goodness, he could be so melodramatic. Why does he have to set the bar so high? Why does he expect so much? Why does he demand *everything*? I thought marriages were supposed to be fifty/fifty.

The picture of Ruthie with her little girl slipped from my fingers. I had forgotten I was still holding it.

How quickly I had forgotten all the sacrifices he had just shown me.

Suddenly, my grievances seemed so petty. I didn't care what it cost—I'd give everything up for this man. He was the best man I'd ever met. He was the best man I would ever find. And he loved *me*. I knew that unquestionably now. I would be better with him than I could ever be alone. What did anything else matter?

"Do you love me?" he asked a third time. "Do you trust me to do what's best for both of us?"

"Okay, I surrender." I could feel myself letting go of all control, the weight of my many burdens slipping from my shoulders. "I still don't know why you are selling the house and giving away your inheritance instead of fighting, but whatever you want to do, I'm with you. I trust you,... and I love you. Your dad was right," I gestured to the evidence of my sin, and his love, all around us. "I have to admit it looks like you love me, too."

A broad smile spread across his face. His eyes sparkled. But instead of taking me in his arms like I expected, he took my hand in his, lifted it to his lips and kissed it. "I have a surprise for you." He raised me to my feet and led me out onto the veranda overlooking the garden.

At the railing, he let go of my hand to put an arm around my waist and spoke in a loud voice to all the guests gathered on the terrace below. "Could I have your attention please? I have an announcement to make."

My heart pounded. What could this be? My head was still spinning with everything I had just learned. Fear fought with my newfound confidence in Josh.

"Abby and I would like you all to be the first to know that we have sold our home and, with the generous help of my father, have purchased the beautiful estate next door."

Next door?

In *this* neighborhood? Purchased it for who?

"This estate will be our new home as well as the home of The Sanctuary, a foundation dedicated to helping women in crisis, headed by our dear friend Ruthie. Ruthie, please come join us as we raise a glass to toast the beginning of this wonderful new partnership."

Ruthie was here? The surprises kept on coming.

But the thing I had been so afraid might be exposed for so long was now known. It was no longer shameful. It was redeemed and beautiful. Not because of anything I had done—except being willing, finally, to let Josh take over. He and his dad both knew how badly I had messed up. They knew even more than I did. But now they were offering me not only forgiveness but absolution.

I thought Josh had given his inheritance to Ruthie, but he gave his inheritance to absolve me of my guilt. He'd given everything for *me*.

I turned toward him, stepping into his embrace, and he leaned down and kissed me in front of everyone. "I don't know how to thank you," I murmured as I buried my head into his neck.

"Lift up your head, Abby," he said softly. "Everything I have is yours, sweet girl. It always has been. I want so much more for you than squabbling over scraps with Ruthie or anyone else."

"Anyone else would have given up on me. I was selfish and greedy. I brought shame on myself and our family."

He stopped me with another quick kiss and wiped away a stray tear. "You are my beautiful bride. Precious to me." As he looked at my face, the corners of his mouth turned up in a wide grin. "I won't tolerate anyone tearing down my beloved, including you."

Seeing his genuine delight, the crippling weight of shame that had been squeezing the life out of me rolled off my shoulders like someone had cut the straps with a knife. I could stand up tall, confident, and free.

"Okay. Let's go home." I pulled his hand away from the balcony railing.

"I can't wait to show you our new home!" He laughed as he twirled me around. "But first, let's celebrate! This is a party after all."

O, Corel!

There will be much rejoicing in the heavens tonight. Hallelujah! Glory to God in the Highest! Our girl is safe at last!

You did it, my brother! She is back in her beloved's arms. The mission is a resounding success! Seeing him twirling her around ... I don't think anything could be more beautiful than the joy in their faces—and made more precious for being so dearly bought. I can't think about it without crying tears of thankfulness.

All that time, Abby was trying to hide her sin, excusing it, judging others, trying to forget it or deny it. Our Enemy tricks them into fearing the very thing that will give them relief—confession and absolution. Did you see how she blossomed when she finally realized she was known and loved anyway?

Congratulations, holy warrior and skilled Guardian! You stepped in at just the right moment! As Abby knelt before her father-in-law, we all saw Twisttale leading the legion of demons to attack, ready to devour her soul. Perhaps you heard us cheering and encouraging you.

"Now, Corel. NOW!" Our shouts were so loud, I was surprised the party-goers didn't hear them!

Or maybe you, like we, simply knew the moment had come to throw up your shield of faith to block their flaming arrows and wrap Abby in the cloak of your protection.

Still, the enemy bore down, baring their razor-sharp teeth, underestimating the power of a single heavenly combatant. But you, brave warrior, stood your ground. Did you see their demonic faces twist in horror when you pulled back your outer cloak, brandished your sword of the Spirit, and reflected the glory of God? Only a small glimmer of God's glory proved more than enough for them and sent them fleeing blindly away.

As much as I loved that moment, perhaps my favorite was watching you with your dagger of truth deftly freeing her from that web of lies that has kept her bound for so long—snapping each strand, one at a time, as she rose from the floor of the study, as she made her way through the party toward Josh, as they went through each item in the box. You cut through each and every deception.

And then, with that final glorious blow, she stood beside her husband on the balcony, and it all fell away, leaving her finally free to embrace the full meaning of forgiveness and the abundant life of grace and hope, twirling and dancing in her husband's arms!

I'm going to need a minute to compose myself after all the excitement and celebration here in Heaven, but I did want to answer your question. You asked why Abby was so important to the Kingdom of Heaven. Why would we pull the mighty sword of one of our greatest warriors from the battle in the Heavenly realm to work on earth? Yes, my dear Corel, you guessed it correctly. Abby is a child of God. His beloved daughter. She is not His only child, but each one is immeasurably precious to him.

With eternal joy in His Glory and love and admiration for you,

Ariam

Damn you! Damn you! Damn you!

I can scarcely begin to express my loathing for you, Stumbletrick, you incompetent moron! I would rip your head off, but that would be too quick. Thankfully, there's no need for me to waste my stinking breath or dirty my claws on your pathetic corpse. Our tormentors below have more ways than I do to make you wish you weren't an eternal being and could feel the relief of death. You will soon receive your just reward for your pathetic performance. I hope never to see your grotesque face on this continent again. If there is any silver lining in this worst of all outcomes, it's perhaps Our Father Below will see that the ways of the East and demons like yourself have no place here and will give me more of a free hand.

And I can't even believe that you have the audacity to claim that I also fled from the Guardian in the decisive moment. Don't ever let me hear of you repeating that filthy lie or questioning my decisions again! I made a strategic retreat based on the chaos caused by the cowardice of all you lesser demons. Even as you were fleeing in terror, I sent a last flaming arrow that almost saved the day, but you wouldn't have seen that as you were trampling over one another, skin burning, eyes blinded trying to get away from that terrible light. Despite the catastrophic failure on your part, I'm not willing to concede this soul just yet. I've worked too hard to lay the groundwork.

I'll lure her back.

This is not the final battle. The American church left her first love once before. I can get her to do it again.

It's not over until the lake of fire—

Twisttale

Epilogue

MICAH LEYDORF

ABBY'S JOURNAL

Wednesday, November 24th —

Who would have thought I would be so happy living in this enormous house with Ruthie and a bunch of strangers? I still pinch myself sometimes.

I am looking down from my window at a Norman Rockwell-worthy scene of doting mothers playing with their adorable children under a canopy of brilliant red, orange, and gold autumn leaves. I never knew life could be filled with such beauty, peace, and joy.

But the real miracle is Ruthie. She helped the girls plan a surprise half-birthday party for me last night! How does a person who could hardly stand the sight of me, and who I was so angry with I couldn't see straight, get to the point where she would voluntarily make me an Italian cream cake? I don't even know how many steps it takes to get that recipe right.

But that's where we are—sitting out on the porch after dinner and chatting about the joys and challenges of the day instead retreating to our rooms and staring at screens. I still mess up occasionally, and so does she. But remembering how bad things were helps—me at least—to keep on showing up, being honest, and giving others grace and respect.

With all there is to do at The Sanctuary, I don't have much time to get together with Eden and Ivy anymore, and Jessica seems like a new woman! Life in the house with all the other new moms definitely agrees with her. Her daughter Mercy is just about the most beautiful thing I've ever seen—with those perfect little ringlets around her chubby cherub face and that sweet smile you can't help but return.

It would be easy to forget the hard times, but you know what they say about those who don't remember the past being condemned to repeat it. I don't want to go back there, of course. Ever. Especially now knowing the joy and peace available when I reject the lies and embrace the truth.

I've never been so in love—with tiny newborn babies curled up on my chest at night while I give their mamas a break, with children laughing while they play freeze tag in the garden, with Ruthie singing in the kitchen or praying before our meals. Destiny drops by when she is home from college to help with the babies, and Cash seems to enjoy helping his dad and granddad with all the projects at the homes of the new mothers. Sometimes I think I might die of gratitude.

And Josh? It's hard to remember why I doubted his goodness. He's the center of my world. We start every morning together with coffee on our bedroom balcony before the rest of the house rises. Every beautiful vista in this rambling old house reminds me that he did this. He created this life for me. This wasn't my dream. I never could have imagined something like this for myself. It's too big. It's too wonderful. I see the large homes that I once drooled over as sterile showplaces big enough for our family to lead separate lives. What we needed were open hearts and a kitchen and dining room table big enough to always squeeze in just one more. At night, I lie in his arms as he tells me about his joys and sorrows of the day, and I tell him about mine.

I framed all those pictures, the ones in the box. They hang on our bedroom wall in case I forget, in case this house isn't enough to remind me of his love and all that he sacrificed for me. I thrive in supporting the work of The Sanctuary and helping our many dear friends here.

I try not to let the whispers in anymore—voices that feed into my fears. I still hear them, but most of the time, I cut them off more quickly now, and I spend less time on social media. Of course, occasionally, I'll slip back into my old patterns.

Only last week I had gotten caught up in my thoughts again, letting myself get drawn into an imagined drama going on around me—among the girls, with Ruthie, with Josh—weaving together scenarios that, if allowed to fester, would create resentment, jealousy, and anger.

But tonight, Josh sat on the porch waiting for us when we came out after cleaning up from dinner. He invited me to join him on the loveseat. He wrapped his arms around me and pressed his head against my hair briefly and then turned his attention to one of the newest girls to arrive at the house, who was sitting in the porch swing nearby.

"Leslie, please tell us your story."

She complied as no one can resist that sincere manner of his. We followed his lead—listening to her tell about her life the way she saw it. When she paused, we joined her in the silence. We later asked questions intended to make visible and known the hard parts we are all tempted to hide.

When she was done, I could see through my own preconceived notions and imagined slights to experience her story of suffering in a way that did not cast judgement on her mistakes. I could also see the beauty beginning to emerge in its aftermath. We understood more clearly her sharp edges and silently granted her more grace.

"Thank you for that," I said when we were in bed that night. "Thank you for helping me not to stray too far, for helping me to see her the way you see her."

At my oblique confession, he smoothed my hair with his hand. I remembered all too well when I would have interpreted the quiet as his silent judgment. Now, I glanced up at the photos on the wall, leaned a little more heavily against him, and waited for him to respond.

Oh yes, I'll happily drink this cup.

MICAH LEYDORF

Postscript

No allegory is perfect, and this one is no exception.

The American church is far from Christ's only love.

Embrace the truth where you see it.

Don't let imperfections distract you where you don't.

May you see yourself, whoever you are,

as a beloved child of God, the bride of Christ,

bought with a price,

loved beyond measure,

and empowered for the work of bringing His kingdom on Earth.

Because that is the Truth.

Peace to you.

Want More?

Wait, what?!

Josh and Abby are actually an allegory for Jesus Christ and his bride, the American church? Yes!

Their story is not only about a single man and woman but chock-full of deeper truths about the lies of Satan that the American Church has believed? Yes!

The final chapter is a depiction of the greatest love story ever told—God's unfathomable love for us—and the tragedy that we don't see it? Yes!

Don't worry, we won't leave you with this new revelation, but no one to discuss or explore it with! **Go to micahleydorf.com/surprise to receive an additional study guide** which will help you re-examine the story from this new perspective either individually or in a group.

TO REVIEW:

Please DO go to micahleydorf.com/surprise to receive the additional study guide.

Please DO join the conversation and discuss the implications of the allegory with others.

But please DON'T spoil the surprise for those in the process of reading it. This second study guide was intentionally excluded from the book to allow everyone the fun of discovering the allegory on their own if they wish.

MICAH LEYDORF

Group Study Questions

Chapter 1 – Surprise Party

Can you relate to Abby and Josh's struggle? Have you ever tried your best to please someone only to fall short? How did you resolve that conflict?

Do you agree with Twisttale's assertion that humans are incapable of distinguishing fiction from reality? What lies have you heard whispered in your ear? How/when did realize they were lies?

Twisttale isn't the only one aware of the importance of narrative. Ariam tells Corel, *"Far from inconsequential or innocuous, stories can transform the routine into the holy, the ordinary into the sacred."* What story do you use to make sense of the world?

Chapter 2 – The Happiness Project

Abby's life coach tells her to pay attention to what she pays attention to. What do you think that means? What are you paying the most attention to?

Twisttale says the demons use different methods of torture and temptation in the West versus the East. What do you think are some of the most effective Western temptations?

Ariam tells Corel, *"Our Lord sometimes paints His most glorious pictures with dark colors."* Do you believe that is true? Have you seen it happen?

Chapter 3 – Lucas

When and how do you think it's appropriate to discuss your marriage (or other relationships) with others? How should you or do you decide who to let speak into your relationships?

Twisttale says, *"We don't have to whip her around 180 degrees when nudging her two degrees off course plus a little time might suffice to send her far from her desired destination."* Can you think of small compromises in your life that have resulted in taking you far off course?

Chapter 4 – Ivy

Do you have judgmental or know-it-all people in your life like Ivy? How do they affect the way you view the world and others? How do you counteract any negative influence?

In this chapter, Abby recalls meeting Josh's family and his proposal and Ariam talks about the beauty of God reflected in His creation (marriage, sex, food, and children). Which of these images resonated most with you and why? Dostoevsky famously wrote, "Beauty will save the world." Can you remember a time in your life when you felt irresistibly drawn to beauty?

Have you ever thought about the strategic importance of marriage and community as a defense against the forces of evil? How might thinking about them that way change one's behavior?

Chapter 5 – Eden

Do you think Ariam and Twisttale are overstating the importance of Abby's habits and indulgences? Does God really care about what TV shows we watch or what we do with our leisure time?

Twisttale advises Stumbletrick to remember that *"comparison is the thief of joy"* when Abby compares Andrew to Josh. Have you ever been tempted to compare your spouse to another or robbed yourself of joy in another way by comparing what you had to what someone else had?

Twisttale describes multiple ways to keep humans trapped in their sins. Which resonated most with you?

-- tricking them into believing they can't get out
-- frightening them with what would happen if they got out
-- fooling them by giving them the wrong key to get out
-- convincing them they don't want to get out at all,
   ie. the prison of comfort

Chapter 6 – Victor

Abby calls her relationship with Lucas a "Coke" relationship—something she found totally unappealing after she left—and Twisttale berates Stumbletrick for thinking he could lure her with that particular bait. Are there sins from your past that you have been so freed / healed from that you wonder how they ever trapped you in the first place?

Abby is afraid to voice her true thoughts and emotions about her single years aloud to her life coach for fear they do not conform to the socially-acceptable narrative. Have you ever hidden your true feelings on an issue for that reason? How do you think that affected you?

Do you think American women (and men) have been sold a counterfeit to God's perfect plan? If so, how?

Chapter 7 – Subterfuge

Twisttale advises Stumbletrick to tempt Abby with less-obvious sins, like coveting instead of adultery. Can you think of other sins that fly under our radar, so to speak, that we or our culture don't realize or recognize? What are they?

Does the way Twisttale describes Abby's addiction to social media and her phone as bondage make you re-think your own or your family's usage? If so, what are some ways you might be able to temper it?

Which of your sins do you think is most troublesome? Which do you think concerns God the most? Are they the same?

Chapter 8 – Operation Heritage

The demons and angels give us a lot to think about in this chapter as they discuss an otherworldly view of American history. Was there a particular part that stood out to you? An old adage says, "The truth irritates before it liberates." Consider why you might or might not have been offended by the dialogue or opinions expressed in this chapter.

Have you heard or held some of the views expressed in this chapter? Were you raised to view America as exceptional or a Christian nation? Has it ever been difficult for you to separate your love of God from love of country?

Have you ever heard the saying "the perfect is the enemy of the good" before? What do you think it means? Do you agree with Ariam that being good can be a trap keeping humans from being what they are called to be— perfect and holy?

Chapter 9 – Jessica

Can you relate to Abby's struggle to respond to Jessica's pregnancy? Have you ever struggled to balance staying true to your convictions with compassion for someone facing an ethical dilemma?

Twisttale advises convincing Abby that her strengths are her weaknesses and her weaknesses are her strengths. Have you ever been deceived or shamed into thinking your strengths were actually your weaknesses?

Ariam says of Abby's depression and the pills by her bed that, "Sometimes medicine fixes a problem, and sometimes it only cut the wires to the warning lights." Do you think that's true?

Is the traditional family of a husband, wife, and children God's perfect plan for humans? If so, what does that mean for people outside of that structure? Does He love them less?

Chapter 10 – Ruthie

Ariam wonders if "perhaps one day Abby might pray, 'Bless you, lawsuit,' as Alexander Solzhenitsyn said of the Gulag, 'Bless you prison,...'" Have you ever, in retrospect, thanked God for something that seemed like a huge blow at the time? What good came from your hardship?

Do you relate to Abby's sense of betrayal? Do you think she's justified or over-reacting?

Chapter 11 – Josh

Stumbletrick talks about inflicting wounds when humans are young and Abby not even understanding why she reacts so strongly to Ruthie's lawsuit and Josh's comments about it. Are there things you recognize as "triggering" to wounds you received in your formative years?

Chapter 12 – Storming Brewing

Gluttony isn't something we talk about a lot in the West, yet Twisttale seems to think it is as powerful as other sins if not more so. He writes that it is at the heart of "the original sin—desiring to possess, craving to taste, coveting the forbidden." Is the sin of gluttony something that you recognize in your own heart? If so, how is it manifested (in food, shopping, bingeing watching, something else)?

In this chapter, Abby acknowledged a small truth—that Ruthie had helped her and been her friend. Twisttale is furious. Can you relate to that? Is there a time in your life when you had a small but powerful revelation of truth that helped you pierce through a lie you had believed?

Abby is conflicted about how to help her friend Jessica when she doesn't agree with the morality of her decision. How do you decide where to draw the line in supporting and loving someone when you don't agree with their choices?

What do you think of Ariam's assertion that Abby thinks she's better than better than Ruthie? If you're honest, do you think you're better than others? Who?

In this chapter, Abby mentions that Ruthie and Josh are both minorities. As a reader, how did you picture these characters in your mind? Why do you think you pictured them that way?

Chapter 13 – Shirley

What did you think of Twisttale's criticism of Abby's church? Does it ring true or seem too harsh to you?

Who in your life does Shirley remind you of?

What do you think of her advice? Twisttale says face-to-face confrontation is the only way out of their conflict. Do you agree? Do you sometimes avoid hard conversations by substituting email or text? Or ignoring the situation all together?

Chapter 14 – Ash Wednesday

What do you think of Abby's apology? What makes a good apology? Abby likes to say she did her best. Is trying one's hardest good enough?

Ariam talks about Abby's visit helping to cut through the enemies' webs of deception. What deception do you think she was referring to?

Can you relate to Twisttale's description of using shame and condemnation or false guilt as weapons? Shame is a general feeling of not being good enough as opposed to guilt which is in response to a specific action. Where have shame or self-condemnation influenced your own behaviors?

Chapter 15 – Guess Who's Coming to Dinner

Both the angels and the demons gave great weight to Abby's interaction with the old woman in the grocery store. Have you ever performed or been the recipient of an act of mercy or generosity that powerfully affected you? Did it change the way you viewed the person? How?

Twisttale writes, *"Isn't it astonishing the kind of moral pretzels pride and haughtiness make possible? 'I'm such a good, loving person that I will hate for you.'"* What kind of moral pretzels does this bring to mind? Have you seen this happen? Have ever been tempted to "hate" for a good cause?

The infamous dinner hardly goes as planned. Who could have caused it to go differently? What could they have done?

Chapter 16 – A Place of Power

Abby thinks that forgiveness and unconditional love are unrealistic pipes dreams, so she keeps her worst sins a secret. Have you ever felt that no one would love you if they knew the worst thing you'd done?

On the other hand, have you ever felt the joy of confessing and receiving forgiveness for something you thought was unforgiveable? If so, how did you find the courage to admit your fault and ask for forgiveness?

How do you view suffering? As a punishment? Something to avoid at all costs? As humans, we acknowledge a certain level of pain and discomfort as necessary for growth in athletics, education, or other areas, but not usually our spiritual life or in our relationships. How would your behavior change if you accepted suffering as sanctifying in other areas? How do you distinguish between sanctifying suffering and abuse?

What did you think of the little church where Abby's car stalled out? Who do you think emptied Abby's gas tank?

Chapter 17 – Take Me to Church

Abby describes the little church as a place for broken people. Have you ever been to a place like that? Would you feel comfortable there? Do you feel like you can reveal your brokenness at your church or in your faith community?

Do you have a friend like Shirley who you can trust to give you sound advice rather than tell you what you want to hear? Are you a friend like that to someone else?

What do you think of Twisttale's description of American churches? Remember, demons aren't always trustworthy narrators. What parts do you think are true?

Can you relate to Abby's falling into Twisttale's trap of "speaking the truth in love?" Have you ever thought you were doing the right thing, even the hard thing, only to later discover you had been deceived? Do you find yourself critiquing others more often than examining your own heart?

Chapter 18 – Girls Night Out

The Bible says things like "The Lord detests all the proud of heart," (Proverbs 16:5) and lists pride among the things God hates the most. How does God's attitude toward pride differ from most Americans' view of pride?

What do you think is Abby greatest sin? Ariam tells Corel it is no small feat to cut through the web of deception that has hidden Abby's sin and disguised it as virtue. What virtue might Abby's sin be disguised as?

Twisttale states, "*Our Divine Enemy has the hard job—trying to transform [humans] into something they are not.*" We can't always trust demons to express an accurate view of the world. Do you agree with his assessment in this case? Why or why not?

Chapter 19 – Guess Who's Coming to Church

Abby was terrified to enter Ruthie's church but later questions why. What do you think Abby's greatest fear was? Have you ever been afraid of something but after confronting it questioned why? When?

Can you relate to the cycle from sin to self-righteousness that Twisttale describes? How do you see that reflected in your own life?

When Abby confronts and accuses Josh of betrayal, he claims he loves her and asks her to trust him. Are Josh's actions loving? Would you trust him? Have you ever felt deeply betrayed by someone you loved? How do you determine whether or not you can trust them?

Chapter 20 – Porch Confessions

What did you think of Ruthie's revelation? Were you surprised?

Ruthie exposes a sin so great that Abby couldn't even admit it to herself. *"We might not have spoken the words, even to one another, but her baby's blood was on my hands as much, if not more, than it was on hers."* Fear of this sin's exposure had hung like a weight over Abby's head for years, yet what happened when she finally faced it and admitted her guilt? Have you ever experienced the liberation of confession and forgiveness for a grievous wrong you committed?

Ariam writes to Corel, *"I love how you wasted no time in landing a powerful blow on that sneaky demon when Abby finally prayed. You sliced right through that veil that had been blinding both of them from seeing each other as God sees them. Oh, it was so beautiful—to see them both beholding one another as the immortal souls they are, starting on a mutual path toward redemption and love."* Do you believe that our prayers empower angels to act in our defense?

Chapter 21 – Surprised by Grace

This chapter is jam-packed full of symbolism. What elements do you see? Which part or parts resonated with you the most? Why?

You can read this book as simply a story about an individual woman, but, as Twisttale reveals in his last letter, it can also be read as an allegory–a story within a story that reveals a deeper truth. If Abby represents the American church in the allegory, who do the other characters represent? Did you see Josh's father as our loving Heavenly Father, Shirley as the Holy Spirit, or Abby's friends as influences on the American church like materialism, intellectualism, and hypersexualization? How about Ruthie as historically disenfranchised people groups that the American church has not always seen as their equal?

Do you think Satan tempts men and women differently? How about different countries or cultures? What do you think are some of the ways he has deceived the American church (church in the universal sense, not a specific denomination or individual congregations, but American Christian believers as a whole)?

MICAH LEYDORF

Acknowledgements

Writing this book has been a long circuitous journey, and I am so grateful for the many people who have offered a hand or insight along the way.

Thanks are owed to C.S. Lewis and his genius *Screwtape Letters* which inspired my first draft so many years ago.

The book would not have been written without the support and encouragement of my husband Tom, originally a skeptic, who quickly became the book's biggest cheerleader and advocate after reading initial sketches.

My beloved fiction critique group led by amazing editor and author Robin Patchen helped shape the book into the story it is today—providing invaluable feedback as it transformed over the years from mere demon letters to a full-fledged novel complete with plot, characters, redemption, and eventually a surprise allegorical meaning woven throughout.

Inspiration and insights also came from psychiatrist, author, and friend Curt Thompson, particularly *The Soul of Shame* and *Anatomy of the Soul*.

Writing this book has been an act of obedience, and I have always known that both writing it and putting it out into the world were not something I could do in my own strength. Only God could do those things. So I am grateful for every beta reader, each pilot book group member, and all my prayer partners. I view each word of encouragement, every hand offered, and all the prayers lifted as sweet gifts from God. Thank you, dear friends, for being his hands and feet and soliciting His aid.

Made in the USA
Middletown, DE
25 March 2024

51809589R00177